SUZANNE

ANAÏS BARBEAU-LAVALETTE

translated by RHONDA MULLINS

Coach House Books, Toronto

First English edition, second printing. Originally written by Anais Barbeau-Lavalette and published in French as *La femme qui fuit* by Marchand de feuilles, 2015.

Published with the generous assistance of the Canada Council for the Arts and the Ontario Arts Council. Coach House Books also acknowledges the support of the Government of Canada through the Canada Book Fund.

LIBRARY AND ARCHIVES CANADA CATALOGUING IN PUBLICATION

Barbeau-Lavalette, Anaïs, 1979-
[Femme qui fuit. English]
    Suzanne / by Anaïs Barbeau-Lavalette ; translated by Rhonda Mullins.

Translation of: La femme qui fuit.
ISBN 978-1-55245-347-6 (softcover).--ISBN 978-1-77056-507-4 (EPUB).--
ISBN 978-1-77056-508-1 (PDF).--ISBN 978-1-77056-509-8 (Kindle)

    I. Mullins, Rhonda, 1966-, translator II. Title. III. Title: Femme qui fuit. English

P S 8603.A705F4513 2017   c843.6   c2017-900550-2

Suzanne is available as an ebook: ISBN 978 1 77056 507 4 (EPUB), ISBN 978 1 77056 508 1 (PDF), ISBN 978 1 77056 509 8 (MOBI)

Purchase of the print version of this book entitles you to a free digital copy. To claim your ebook of this title, please email sales@chbooks.com with proof of purchase. (Coach House Books reserves the right to terminate the free digital download offer at any time.)

The first time you saw me, I was one hour old. You were old enough to have courage.

Fifty, maybe.

It was at St. Justine Hospital. I had just come into the world. I already had a big appetite. I drank her milk like I make love now, like it's the last time.

My mother had just given birth to me. Her daughter, her firstborn.

I imagine you entering the room. Your face round like ours. Your dark eyes heavily lined in kohl.

You enter unapologetically. Walking confidently. Even though it has been twenty-seven years since you last saw my mother.

Even though twenty-seven years ago you ran away. Leaving her there, teetering on her three-year-old legs, the memory of your skirts lingering on her fingertips.

You walk calmly toward us. My mother's cheeks are red. She is the most beautiful thing in the world.

How could you just walk away?

How did you not perish at the thought of missing her nursery rhymes, her little-girl lies, her loose teeth, her spelling mistakes, her laces tied all by herself, then her crushes, her nails painted then bitten, her first rum-and-Cokes?

Where did you hide to avoid thinking about it?

Now, there is her, there is you, and between you, there is me. You can't hurt her anymore, because I'm here.

Does she hold me out to you, or do you reach your empty arms toward me?

I end up near your face. I fill the gaping hole in your arms. My newborn eyes search yours.

Who are you?

You leave. Again.

The next time I see you, I'm ten years old.

I am perched at the third-floor window, my breath melting the lacy frost on the pane.

Rue Champagneur is white.

On the other side, a woman falters, her long coat no longer enough to protect her.

Some things children can guess, and even though I don't know you, I sense you in this waltz of hesitation.

You cross the street in long strides, your toes barely landing. A water spider.

You dart, you head toward us, leaving no trace of yourself on the ground.

You slide a small book into the mailbox before slipping off, yet again. But right before you disappear, you look at me. I promise myself I will catch up with you one day.

The train is heading to Ottawa.

I'm twenty-six years old. Beside me, my mother is reading a magazine to keep her mind off things. I like peering over her shoulder at the pictures of girls in dresses.

We have a mission in Ottawa, a city we don't know. We are both looking forward to the end of the day, when we can wander and lose ourselves in neighbourhoods off the beaten path, the sort we love.

But my mother has had an idea. We are going to go see you. If you are still alive, you live in a tower near the Rideau Canal. That was the last place you sent word from.

We can't call because you'll tell us not to come.

We have to show up in person.

But I don't know if I want to. I don't love you.

I'm even a little afraid of you.

In the end, I preferred it when you didn't exist.

My mother is still afraid of being abandoned.

Even though a mother is not someone who can be abandoned, we have to be careful, because it's not all that clear to her.

I ask her whether she is sure she wants to go.

She says yes.

The day goes by, and we find ourselves in a taxi, on our way to you.

Ten identical towers reach toward the sky. A caretaker is in the foyer. The names of tenants are listed on the wall, each one with a little buzzer for visitors to announce their arrival.

Suzanne Meloche. Your name. Written in your hand. Round, painstaking letters. Apartment 560.

We slip in with a neighbour. Outlaws.

We don't talk in the elevator.

Fifth floor. This is it. We walk down the long corridor. We are stationed in front of your door. My mother knocks. We wait. Footsteps. I'm scared.

You open the door.

My young woman's eyes bore into yours, which are stony.

You smile.

You don't miss a beat. You hardly seem surprised.

And yet. The last time we were all together, I was just born.

You open the door a little wider. So we go in. And you ask us to sit down.

My mother and I sit side by side. On alert. Ready to make a run for it if need be.

You are facing us. You must be eighty years old. Prominent cheekbones, thin lips, ebony eyes.

You look like us.

Then you start talking. You look mainly at me. And you wink.

It's the three of us. It's so natural it's disturbing. As if we could just sit in silence and flip through women's magazines together.

In a resonant voice, a voice younger than your years, you tell us about the neighbourhood, which is quiet, safe. The fellow tenants who don't bother you, and Hilda, a neighbour with whom you eat sometimes. You tell us an old woman's tales, but your voice and your eyes are twenty. Your smile too, animated, intense.

Your old-lady words shield you. You string them together while I search for you somewhere else.

Your apartment is small and bright. Books are scattered on the floor, as if forgotten mid-read. They, too, await your return.

In the kitchen, the sink is filled with dirty dishes. You eat alone.

If you had wanted, we could have come to eat with you sometimes. We would have brought quiches, fruit, smoked salmon. My mother would have set the table to avoid tiring you out. She sets the loveliest tables. But you'll never know.

Now you are talking about your brothers. One of them just died. If you are sad, you don't show it.

My mother tells you that she heard from Claire. Your sister who's a nun. You laugh. Your teeth are white and straight, except for one. A rebel. Claire doesn't seem to interest you, but she makes you laugh.

All three of us have the same crooked tooth. Have you noticed?

Then my mother asks why you left.

You don't want to answer: *No! Not that. Not today.*

My mother doesn't insist. We are cloaked in a thick silence. But you, you glide above it. Impenetrable.

I look at you one last time.

You have big breasts. Not us.

You have armour. Not us.

We are together. Not you.

We haven't inherited everything.

My mother decides to leave. She would rather make a break for it before you can hurt us. You never know. Goodbye, Grandmother. You wink at me one last time.

We're going skating on the canal. We're on holiday.

It's cold. We skate holding hands because I'm not a good skater and because we need to. The canal is long and empty. The smooth ice belongs to us. The cold is biting and brings us back to life.

My mother's phone rings. It's you. You tell her not to do that again. You tell her you never want to see us again. Ever.

My mother hangs up. It's not the first time she has had to swallow rejection. All the past ones are still there. Stuck in her throat.

She has learned not to choke on them, but just barely.

She doesn't say a word, but she doesn't let go of my hand. We hold on to each other.

I hate you. I should have told you so to your face.

On the train, I fall asleep against my mother, who is smaller than me.

Then, one day, you die.

Five years later. In the same small apartment where you annihilated me with seven winks.

We are nestled away in the country, this family my parents built, that is nothing like you. A close family.

Claire, the religious sister you would no longer see, calls to tell us you're dead.

My mother leans against the wall. Her stomach is Hiroshima. She is finally rid of your absence.

Maybe she'll start being normal. A woman with a mother who is dead and buried.

But the soft voice at the other end of the line tells us that a few days before you died you wrote your will, and our names are in it. The names of my mother and her brother, then mine and my brother's.

We are your sole heirs. So, finally, you are inviting us over. We have to go empty your little apartment.

We set out into winter to meet you. Through the storm. Archaeologists of a murky life. Who were you?

We are on our hands and knees, searching.

Your closet. Hats. Dresses. Lots of black clothes.

I can't help but plunge my nose into the fabric. Smells are usually so revealing. But here even they are furtive. Subtle, faint, hard to pin down. An accidental blend of incense and the sweat of days spent not moving. A subtle note of alcohol, perhaps?

In a shoebox there are pictures of us: me and my brother, at every age. You kept them. And my mother kept sending them to you year after year. Our ages are written on the back, traces of time lost, wasted, slipped away. It's your loss.

My mother is sitting in your rocking chair. Gently, she touches you. Rests her hands where you rested yours. Rocks to the rhythm of a lullaby, the one she never heard.

I find your red red lipstick in the small bathroom. And short sticks of kohl, which you lined your eyes with, giving them power. I draw a line under mine.

My mother finds a piece of furniture, made by her father a long time ago. We take it down to the car. She takes the rocking chair too, carrying it on her back, and my father lashes it securely to the roof.

We're leaving soon. I'm in your room. There is a small green plant in the window. It is leaning against the pane, drawn by the day.

Books are piled by the foot of your bed. I read a few passages at random, suddenly greedy for clues about you.

I find a yellowed cardboard folder between two books on Buddhist zazen.

It contains letters. Poems. Newspaper articles.

A gold mine, which I stuff into my bag like a thief.

We are leaving. I slip a worn copy of *Thus Spoke Zarathustra* into my pocket.

We close the door behind us, forever.

We drive slowly through the storm. On the roof, the rocking chair cuts through the wind, heroically. I don't know it yet, but I will rock my children in it.

I flip through Nietzsche, yellowed with age. There is a laminated newspaper article stuck between two pages.

The picture of a burning bus.

1961, Alabama.

In bold type: *Freedom riders: political protest against segregation.*

Around the bus are young Black people and White people, in shock, refugees from the flames. A young woman is on her knees. She looks like me.

You had to die for me to take an interest in you.

For you to turn from a ghost to a woman. I don't love you yet.

But wait for me. I'm coming.

The dead are us, that is certain, there is a mysterious link through which our life nourishes itself from theirs.

George Sand

We don't fall from the sky. We grow on our family tree.

Nancy Huston

For my mother,
For my daughter.

1930–1946

Lower Town Ottawa. LeBreton Flats.

Little houses with peeling paint bow their heads, the bells of Saint Anne's church ring, and the men are coming home from the factory with heavy hands and empty stomachs.

It's hot and it smells like wet dirt.

The river is overflowing. It's made it as far as the cemetery this time. The water is above the tombstones. The river has left its bed, lapping at the homes and the feet of the hurried, chasing anything that moves, awakening the dead. You wonder whether coffins are watertight. And you imagine the dead doing breaststroke.

You stand tall on your long legs. Your face is all eyes, and you have jagged bangs that get caught in your eyelashes.

They hide your prominent forehead. Your mother feels as though your brain wants to pop through it. She contains it as best she can, cuts your bangs to form a lid. If she could let you grow them down to your chin, she probably would, to filter your words at least, since she can't control your thoughts.

The water laps at your feet, soaks through your white stockings in your nicely polished shoes. You want to taste it, to see if it tastes like death. You dip your finger in and bring it to your mouth.

Apparently this is why the French cemetery was placed near the water. Because the French don't mind their dead being underwater. The English, well, they would never let that happen.

It is tasteless. You're disappointed.

'Get it! Get it!'

You turn. On the other side of the street, a group of children are chasing a rat.

'Come on, Claire. Let's go!'

You drag your little sister along behind them.

You cross the street, water up to your calves. You don't hear your mother calling, trying to hold you back, again. She lives in hope of succeeding one day.

You take long strides, your face intent. You are off to war.

You dive onto your belly after the rat, which you catch with both hands, holding it firmly, brandishing it like a trophy, your eyes sharp and your face like an animal's.

'Got it!'

Your sister Claire looks at you, impressed. You turn to face the English kids, the rat in hand, your dress dirty. You stare at them, a rebel.

You are four years old.

Mass is starting in five minutes.

You have mud in your underwear.

You look out the window. Walking at a leisurely pace, people are already cramming into the church on the corner. Everyone is clean and pressed, at least down to their knees.

Below the knees, everything is grey and wet.

'Suzanne! Hurry up!'

Claudia, your mother, is calling from downstairs. You finish putting on your white blouse and go down.

Madeleine, Paul, Pierre, Monique, and Claire are clean and waiting sensibly at the door. Your mother is seated, thin and pale. She looks you up and down, severely.

She has given up on words, doesn't even look for them. She hides behind her sharp eyes. Eyes that scrutinize you and condemn you to your core. You avoid them, glide above them.

The dried mud in your underwear itches, but you don't show it.

Your brothers help your mother up, then you leave.

As you walk by, you graze the keys of the old piano with your fingers and gather the dust. Your mother catches you. You're not allowed to touch the piano. You say you're sorry in a clear voice.

You have always had a voice that carries. Even when you whisper. You don't know how to tone things down. Words move through your throat in a coarse, precise stream, a diamond, an arrow.

It's a good piano. A Heintzman, wood. Its front is engraved with scrolls that chase each other, swirling, never meeting.

It came into the house twelve years ago. Claudia, your mother, loved it. She played piano as a teenager. Her aunt taught her scales. Claudia found scales more musical than most pieces and played them one after the other with heartfelt enjoyment. She could have played only scales.

It moved her deeply that the pressure of her slender fingers could make such passionate sounds, filling the space. She liked to touch the piano keys; they gave her power. She felt alive.

Later she took lessons with a woman who wore pretty flowered dresses and sheer stockings with no runs.

With her, Claudia took off her shoes when she played, to feel the crisp cold of the pedals on the soles of her feet.

She played Chopin, because it sounded like the sea.

She had talent.

Then she met Achilles. He was a teacher, knew a great deal and didn't speak much. He had the sort of presence that leaves an impression. Someone you feel has been there several minutes after he leaves. Claudia wanted to swim in his wake, bathe in what overflowed from him.

They got married. They found a big house, on Cambridge Street, in the working-class quarter of Ottawa. It was across the street from the church, which was handy.

Claudia wanted to take her piano with her. Achilles carried it there with his bare hands.

They picked a nice spot for it in the house, so that Claudia could sit there, like a queen on her throne.

But Claudia had her first child and never again sat down at the piano.

When Achilles asked her to play, she would smile inside. An evasive smile.

One day, she simply told him she no longer knew how.

Achilles stayed, waiting for her to go on, and she couldn't get away from him, so she said that she didn't know how to touch the keys, because she had nothing more to give.

That she felt as though the notes would crash into the walls and the ceiling, then fall to the ground.

Achilles was calm and quietly told her that all they had to do was open the windows.

Claudia loved him and cried a little. But she never played the piano again.

The piano still sits enthroned in the middle of the living room. It gathers dust and that annoys her.

One night, you saw her clean it. She rubbed it furiously with a rag. As if it were one big stain.

On Saturdays, you used to go with your mother to the hairdresser's. It was your outing. While she was having her hair curled, lightening up in a way she rarely did, you would line up for the telex. A small, seemingly ordinary machine, but one that helped the poor get rich. People would read stock prices, current up to the minute. The small machine sitting between two permed ladies was wired to Wall Street.

That impressed you.

Your father speculated like everyone else. After carefully noting the numbers on the palm of your hand, you called home and gave them to him.

Often, a few days later, a new oven, fridge, or set of dishes, bought on credit, would find their way into the house.

You deserved to be rich. Like everyone else.

Before, you had your bedroom, which you shared with your sisters. You had your rituals, your secrets, your lair.

You liked to sleep naked, your body in the form of a star, arms and legs open wide on the bed, while on the other side of the wall, the boys fought and snored.

Before, every new year, your father would buy you a pair of new shoes. You would spend a week looking down at them, your neck bent, eyes glued to your shiny new feet.

Then, the crisis.

Your mother went to the hairdresser's once or twice more. But she wouldn't let you check the telex. The stock market didn't seem to interest anyone anymore, and the impatient line had suddenly dispersed.

You had nothing more to do at the salon; you didn't have a mission anymore, and your mother's reflection in the mirror, under the hairdresser's hands, had gone dark.

You had to drag your mattress into the boys' room.

Now you slept crammed together, no more secrets, odours intermingling.

A stranger moved into your room, 'the lodger.' It was by order of the government: a room had to be freed up to make a place for the indigent. The lodger had lost his home. He was soaking up your space, your light, your memories. You didn't like him. He was poor, and he had taken your place.

And then you didn't get new shoes. At the beginning of the year, your mother cleaned a pair that had belonged to your older sister. And they were handed down to you.

That's when you lifted your head. That's when you started to look to the horizon.

Claudia is finishing up ironing your skirt. Sitting in your underwear on a chair, you are focused on the rumbling in your stomach. The hunger comes in waves. Nothing, and then an empty tunnel that opens up between your belly button and your throat.

'Put this on. Let's go.'

You grab your blue skirt. Your mother ironed the pleats, made it look like a fan. It's pretty. You put it on and twirl. You are the wind.

Tables have been set up in the parish hall.

The neighbourhood families are seated, waiting patiently for their soup.

You feel like you're at a restaurant. You try to sit up straight, to be worthy of your outfit.

You can't wait. You like to eat.

You recognize almost all the families around you. They all look dressed up. More than usual. Not to hide their hunger. No, to greet it with dignity. To put it on notice that they aren't afraid of it.

And yet the sound of hungry bodies finally being fed betrays the precariousness of the moment. Under their pristine fabrics, they are all hanging by a thread.

There are no jobs. The stores are deserted; the banks are closed.

The park benches and the libraries are filled. They are the two hotspots for the newly unemployed.

While getting an encyclopedia for a school project, you walk by some twenty men taking refuge in their reading. Your eyes linger on one of them. His five-o'clock shadow, his blue eyes glued to the page. Nothing can come between him and what he is reading. He seizes the words like a wolf seizes its prey. They are practically bleeding. They are no longer a refuge; they are a lifebuoy.

Your eyes move down the man's long legs, which lead to his feet, which are bare, wrapped in newspaper. You're sure he read it with the same intensity before using it as protection. He knows the words he is walking in.

We believe that the main causes of the crisis are moral and that we will cure them through a return to the Christian spirit.

Introduction to the *Programme de restauration sociale* (1933)

Father Bisson has one eyebrow, and you have always wanted to touch it. It looks soft.

It's so hot in the church that his eyebrow is beaded with drops that would make a pretty necklace.

You look at your mother's dry neck, and you imagine her wearing it. The two fine bones of her clavicle as a coat rack. Her neck stiff from being bent. From looking at what has to be washed rather than what is taking to the skies.

You squirm on the bench, which creaks. Up front, the priest is addressing the crowd with conviction.

'Our economic recovery must bring jobs to all of our labourers and the unemployed. If the fervour of prayer, patience with the heat and fatigue, could bring about change, our wishes would come true, but we also need to change our lives so that they are more consistently generous and so that mortal sin, often repeated and rarely regretted, does not destroy most of the kind acts of a given day.'

You are seven years old. According to canon law, you have reached the age of reason, and you have to confess at least once a year.

It's dark in the box. It smells like damp wood. It's comfortable. You sit down. For years you have watched the long queue for the confessional, the bodies lined up, looking stiff.

You always thought that the bodies told a different story while they were waiting. As if they were already being scrutinized, spied on.

You try to think of something to talk about. It's your first time. It's important that he remember you. That he look forward to seeing you again.

You go into the box. You close your eyes, gulp down the warm air around you. You gulp down the vices of those who have been here before you. A fix of weakness.

It's your turn. There are small openings in front of you through which thin shafts of light pass, through which you can make out the man you will be speaking to.

He tells you he is listening.

You want it to last.

He repeats that he is listening. He calls you his child.

You can't find the words you had prepared. So you stand up.

And you want him to remember you.

You're hot. You lean into the screen, study it, look for the man on the other side.

And you stick out your tongue. You drag it slowly over the holes. You look for a path that will take you closer to him. You leave trails of saliva on the varnished wood. You slowly slide your tongue into each slot, and on the other side, he has fallen silent.

You leave the confessional, a splinter between your teeth.

You feel light. He won't forget you.

There is no gas left to fuel the cars.

Achilles attaches his to two horses. They will be his motor.

The idea is not his; it is spreading across the country, ironically called the Bennett buggy, after Canadian prime minister Robert Bedford Bennett, who is one of the people running the country into the ground.

Your father comes home late at night in his Bennett buggy.

You sleep between Monique and Claire. Claire talks in her sleep. A foreign language that sounds like Latin. You shove the end of the sheet in her mouth to shut her up.

Claire is five years old. At age eighteen, she will enter the convent, bound to God for the rest of her life.

The sound of horseshoes downstairs: your father, Achilles, is coming home. The crisis has taken his job. Now he has a make-work job, invented by the government to deal with unemployment, something to keep men from weeping or sleeping at the library. To keep them from overdosing on free time.

Achilles comes home more tired than before. He liked being useful, and make-work jobs change every day but are all in vain.

Today, he picked dandelions. They're a weed; there are a lot of them, everywhere. Enough to keep the men busy for a few weeks.

Achilles must have uprooted five thousand of them. He roamed the city, eyes peeled, looking for yellow flowers. Enough to make a person go mad. Golden streaks everywhere. Achilles has blisters on his hands. He was paid eight cents for his work. He is not unemployed. He earned a living today.

Achilles liked being a teacher.

You love Achilles.

You hear him unhitch the horses from the car; you tear down the stairs and throw yourself at him.

He tells you to go to bed, but you don't obey right away. You know that you still have two chances. You help him feed the horses.

He tells you again to go to bed.

You bring him a damp towel, which he wipes his face with.

You ask him whether you can go with him tomorrow.

He tells you to go to bed.

You know you have to obey this time.

You go upstairs.

Achilles goes into his bedroom and lies down next to Claudia. He lifts her nightgown and touches her thighs. He turns his wife over and seeks brutal refuge in her. Where he is a man. Where he is proud.

Claudia doesn't want to but doesn't say so.

Claudia is thirty-three years old and has five children.

Claudia is a distant cousin of Émile Nelligan.

Claudia has black eyes that arch downward. Waning moons.

Claudia has long fingers that have played Chopin.

Claudia has short nails with dirt under them from the potatoes she peels.

Claudia doesn't sleep anymore.

Claudia knows that she has to have six more children to get the two hundred acres of dirt the government has promised.

Claudia thinks that she already has dirt under her fingernails and doesn't want any more.

Claudia doesn't talk anymore.

Claudia is being smothered by *Nocturnes*.

Claudia doesn't know where to love her children because there is no room left.

Claudia is filled with emptiness.

Claudia is a desert.

Claudia wakes the oldest ones.

Asks them to help set up a pallet in the hallway.

Claudia will sleep next to the piano now.

Away from Achilles's penis.

You've been in line for two hours. The ration card in your clammy hand. You close your fist over it so as not to drop it, or else everyone will go hungry, because of you. You've pictured the scene at least twenty times: the card falling, the wind kicking up and carrying it off. You running after it. The card flying off to the river and throwing itself into it. You hesitating and diving in. The river swallowing you up. You floating with the dead in the cemetery.

You tighten your grip.

Take a few steps forward.

Seven ounces of sugar, seven ounces of butter, one and one-third ounces of tea, five and one-third ounces of coffee. The weekly food ration.

The lady in front of you smells like burnt caramel. Her skirt brushes your face and you like it. You want to sleep under it. Your little head pressed against her fat thighs. Her damp, sweet skin. You would slip your tattered card into her sock for safekeeping. And you would rest a while in the shade of her bottom.

The line moves forward a few steps, and you collide with her feet, apologizing.

As you put the food away, the radio is broadcasting the commentary on the French-Canadian Hilda Strike's one hundred-metre dash at the Olympic Games in Los Angeles.

At the whistle, Hilda is off like an arrow, a projectile; she splits the air, shaking off her adversaries, leaving them in her wake. In just two strides, she is already one metre ahead of her competitors.

You freeze, a bag of sugar in your hands, suspended, caught up in Hilda's flight.

The Meteor from Montreal. The Canadian Comet.

'Suzanne?'

Your mother, annoyed that you're just standing there.

Hilda shatters the world record, she pulverizes her adversaries, she gulps in air as the astonished crowd looks on. 'Hilda! Hilda! Hilda!'

But barely fifteen metres from the finish line, Walsh, the Polish champion, catches up.

The two women are neck and neck!

Walsh gives it the rest of what she's got and beats the French Canadian, barely two strides, just a few inches.

Claudia turns off the radio and suggests you put the rest of the groceries away.

Your eyes are watering. You could picture Hilda sprinting; you imagined her taking flight. She loses and suddenly, here you are, stuck in an ordinary living room, putting away your meagre provisions, with your mother avoiding your eyes.

She doesn't like displays of emotions. She is afraid of getting dragged along in their wake. She never looks a tear in the eye.

To put an end to it, she opens the bag of sugar and holds it out to you, inviting you to dip your finger in. A rare dip you take advantage of. The sugar mixes with the saltiness of the few tears you shed.

You ask your mother where Quebec is.

Your mother points to the living room wall.

'That way, I think.'

You stare at the floral wallpaper.

Which you imagine suddenly split open, torn apart by Hilda Strike's meteoric entrance. In shorts and a tank top, muscular, gleaming with sweat.

A trace of a smile on your face.

One day you'll go to Quebec, where the women run fast.

Learn to express yourself properly and you will never be truly poor.

Achilles Meloche

This morning, you accompany your father, who is getting his hands dirty. He is in the second stage of dandelion picking. They have emptied the downtown of dandelions; now they are going to the edges of the country, where the city spills over.

Sitting beside him in the Bennett buggy, you set your shoulders square with the sky. Achilles likes things straight. When you hunch, his large hand whacks you on the lower back.

He says that Ontario French Canadians are people who stand tall. That's what helps them survive.

Sometimes you purposely hunch so he will touch you.

The car moves forward, pulled by the horses, as rusty as the car itself.

You like driving with Achilles because he talks to you. No: he makes you talk. It's not so much what you say that interests him. But how you say it.

He asks you to describe what you see. He makes you start over until the sentence is perfect. The best words, the best order, the best diction. Polished till it shines.

Even if you're describing something dirty.

Today, Achilles stops the Bennett buggy in front of the Hole, a pile of mouldy, makeshift shelters. The smell of sardines and dried piss hangs in what is left of the air. Music – the Boswell Sisters? – crackles in the distance. A few scattered clotheslines stand watch over the rags of families in survival mode.

The Hole looks like it's a thousand years old, but it's new. The Hole is one of the country's first slums.

Achilles parks his Bennett there and won't let you avert your eyes. He wants you to look at it.

He wants you to find words you don't know to describe it.

You say: wood, scrap iron, horror. You say: rat, laughter, music. And then: sad, wet, end of the world.

A child is walking barefoot through the mud.

You say: 'Daddy, I want to leave.'

Achilles asks you what you're afraid of.

He won't budge until you figure it out. Your six-year-old mind tries to put your finger on what is scaring you.

The little boy holds out his hand to you. He wants money. You look down at your lap.

You say you don't know where to look, that everywhere you look you make the misery worse, you make it more real.

The little boy is still holding out his dirty hand to you.

You grab on to your father, beg for his help. Which he denies you.

So you take the little's boys hand in yours. And you introduce yourself using your school voice: 'My name is Suzanne.'

The little boy pulls away from you, running off into the meanderings of the Hole.

Your father hails his old team of horses, which sets off again.

He is satisfied.

You have dipped your tongue in dirt.

You leave the Hole and those rotting in it behind you. But there is an aftertaste of shit and lives with pieces missing.

That's what he wanted.

He wanted you to taste it, to feel sick to your stomach, so that you would do anything to not end up there.

A field of dandelions. Twenty or so men already hard at work. You hike up your skirt and get out of the car. You follow your father, who says hello in English to his brothers in misfortune.

And you get down to work. You have to uproot the flower, attack it by the root. You want to be good; you work with both hands.

Around you, the men are talking about this and that. English mixes with French. The vacant lot is soon rid of dandelions.

A man watches you work. His eyes on your skin. A refuge for his virility. A space to be male in.

Your eyes search for your father, focused, quieter than the others.

He is piling the dandelions to burn them, a bit of him burning along with them. He is already disconnected from you.

Your fingers turn yellow.

You can't count on anyone. You should learn to run.

You used to like dandelions. You made bouquets with them in the spring. You thought it was a valiant flower, the first to grow, the first to brave what remained of winter.

A simple flower, without pretence. You liked it before it became the object of a make-work project. Before it made your father bitter.

You rip out the flowers with violent precision. You are avenging your father.

At the end of the day, a mountain of dandelions is burning. Even the fire isn't pretty. It doesn't even inspire the pride of a job well done. Just black smoke, sadly pointless.

You leave.

The Bennett buggy moves lazily along the dirt roads toward home. You glance at the Hole as you go by.

You wonder whether Hilda Strike could have been born there.

And the idea comes to you that maybe she could have beaten Walsh if she had learned to run barefoot in the mud.

You fall asleep on Achilles's warm shoulder. His silence calms you.

It's cold and people are hungry. People don't want children when they're cold and hungry.

The first family planning clinic opens near you in 1932. A young woman, Elizabeth Bagshaw, decides that her kitchen will become an information counter for women who are exhausted. Young women with bags under their eyes line up, their children in a constellation around them.

Elizabeth explains how to use a condom. They blush, giggle bashfully. They still have to convince their husbands.

You are sitting on the balcony when, one morning, the police show up and take her away. She never comes back to your neighbourhood.

You will remember her wrists in handcuffs, her intelligent eyes, her round bottom, and her deep voice. In that order.

January 30, noon. You are eight years old.

While Adolf Hitler is named Chancellor of Germany, your mother gives birth to her seventh child.

Apparently Achilles managed to thrust his penis into her, and now she is screaming to expel a newborn.

You are pacing back and forth in the living room.

Claudia pants. Giving birth is the only time she makes noise. That may be why Achilles still wants to give her children. Because that's how he knows she's alive. That she sweats, that she smells, that she screams.

Afterward, she will go quiet again.

You place your fingertips on the piano. You're not allowed to. It hurts her.

But you like the forbidden.

You press down on a key, and a note reverberates through the house, impertinent.

A beat. Claudia is moaning in the bedroom.

You press down on another key. Then another.

You know that she can't get up. You would like to play her a symphony. You press your whole hands on the piano keyboard; you grab notes by the fistful, you leave none of them in peace. They belong to you for a moment, and you embrace them.

You press your arms, and then your stomach, against the keys, then you sit your bare thighs on the cold keyboard; you want to warm it up, you want to warm yourself up. You climb onto the piano. You crawl along the keys, and you feel like a giant.

From the bedroom, crying: It's a boy.

From the bedroom, yelling: Claudia says she's going to kill you.

You like school. Mainly for a bizarre reason: you like watching people from behind. Watching their necks. You sit in the back of the class, because the steep slope of anonymous necks reminds you of how fragile they are. From behind, it's as though the crack is inevitable.

Imagining their necks broken brings you closer to others.

In art class, the teacher tries to teach you to trace an apple and a hat.

You wonder about the significance of the pair. Why an apple and a hat?

You have to use a ruler, a compass, and an eraser. You have to, the teacher says.

You apply yourself.

You are a good student.

When you're done, the perfect hat is alongside the perfect apple. You look at your perfect drawing. Your mother will probably hang it on the living room wall.

You think it could use a bit of colour.

You have a hangnail on your right hand. You pull on it. It bleeds a little. You spread the blood on the apple and the hat.

There. Perfect and red. Perfect and bloody.

The teacher is furious. You, so proper, so perfect.

He rips up your work and sends you to the hallway to think about what you've done.

Standing in front of the window, you count the pigeon droppings piled between you and the outdoors. You tell yourself that life is dirty, and that's the way you like it.

You are all gathered at the kitchen table, which your mother is finishing up clearing.

English kids are playing hockey in front of the house, their war cries filtering indoors, and you are told to stop fidgeting. It's time for the family catechism.

Today Achilles tells the story of original sin, of freedom put to the test.

There are eight of you standing around the table, because it's harder to fall asleep when you're standing.

When he starts talking about God, Achilles's face changes. It always makes you smile. He becomes a teacher again. He is focused, doing his best to articulate precisely. He takes refuge in this family sermon, where he still feels useful. You don't know whether he really believes what he is saying, but he throws himself into it, unshakeable, whole.

Claudia listens, nodding her head, eyeing each of her children, making sure they're paying attention. She is the only one who is seated. Her legs could give out from under her. Claudia could collapse at any moment.

Achilles clears his throat, lifts his chin slightly, and begins: 'God created man in his image and established him in his friendship. A spiritual creature, man can live this friendship only in free submission to God. The prohibition against eating of the tree of the knowledge of good and evil spells this out: "for in the day that you eat of it, you shall die."'

Your sister Claire eats up his words; they hold her spellbound. She even seems a little scared.

You are already getting impatient. Blood is running down your legs. You are the promise of a woman. You like the idea. It's a territory you want to explore.

You are stuck at the end of the table. The wooden corner grazes the spot between your legs.

'Man is dependent on his Creator, and subject to the moral norms that govern the use of his freedom. Man, tempted by the devil, let his trust in his Creator die in his heart and, abusing his freedom, disobeyed God's command.'

Achilles continues, his voice deeper.

'Scripture portrays the tragic consequences of this first disobedience. After that first sin, the world is virtually inundated by sin ...'

You press up against the table and it feels good.

Your mother leaps up, overturning the table with her momentum. You jump. Your sister Claire cries out.

Achilles, his sermon interrupted, becomes vulnerable again. He carefully rights the table, looking at his wife, a question in his eyes.

Claudia stares at you. She smooths her skirt, her hands trembling, and apologizes to Achilles in a meek voice, never taking her eyes off you. Calling for him to continue, she suggests with a controlled gesture that you leave the table and sends you to the pots and pans.

You are heading toward the parish, dragging a burlap sack behind you. There are three pots in it. Your mother is doing her part for the coming war. She is making a worthy donation of her pots. There is a real need for aluminum: her pots will become a warship.

You are proud to be a cog in this bit of alchemy.

Plus, it gives you hope. You imagine a pot slicing through the waves and destroying the enemy instead of hanging around in the oven.

One day, you too will turn into a warship.

You walk along the street; your legs have never been so long. You are fourteen, the age of possibility, when we think we are immortal.

Your feet don't touch the ground. You skim it and propel yourself elegantly through the space around you, claiming it as your own.

You reign over the world with a light touch, with disarming assurance.

You enter the classroom, greet your teacher with a sincere smile, and take your seat at the front.

It's oral presentation day, and you have been chosen to get things rolling, which you like doing.

'We are at war,' you say, solemnly.

You are wearing lipstick. You thought that talking about war would be the perfect opportunity to wear lipstick.

You get the distinct impression that the words coming out of your mouth are cushioned. The news is powerful, but your telling of it seems delicate. You choose your words carefully. You pick them with your fingertips, but they settle in your mouth authoritatively and come out ornate, as if proud of having been chosen.

The whole class is hanging on your words. They already know, they are learning nothing new, but they are captivated by the way you honour the language.

'William Lyon Mackenzie King intends to mobilize the Canadian armed forces and the economy to support the war effort. But in September, he announced that he wouldn't necessarily introduce the draft. At the time, our prime minister said he was sensitive to the opinion of French Canadians about the draft. We are still against it. Despite that, this morning, he did an about-face … and announced the mobilization of all single men in three days.'

As you leave school, you hear the church bells ring. Everything seems a little off. An agitated chaos has descended on the city.

At first glance, the church square looks like a cruise ship. A hundred families are milling about in colourful outfits, their gestures random, their laughter nervous.

You stop, trying to understand the scene. Then you spot the two priests, attempting to put order to the milling masses.

Your eyes sharpen and you see the patched, repurposed grooms-wear.

The clothes have been hauled out from parents' chests. They have put a dress over a nightgown that more or less matches. It's a group wedding. There are only a few hours left to get married. A few hours to avoid going to war.

On a table, hard, white cake is set out, made with sugar ration coupons hastily begged from the extended families of the impromptu brides and grooms.

Aware of their power, the priests are running around and feeling useful like never before. They are dispensing *for better or for worse* and savouring the chaste kisses of those plucked from danger.

You watch the spineless, candy-coated crowd. Too much lace, too much laughter, too much happiness.

You tell yourself that if you had the choice, you would choose war.

Cries of joy merge and combine with the blackout siren that sounds through the neighbourhood.

They are playing war games: it's a rehearsal.

People are not scared of it yet. The siren drowns out the music and the church bells.

You need to seek shelter; it's to practise. The cloud of newlyweds slowly disperses. You take cover in the church. The confessional is empty, and you settle in there to wait for the all-clear.

The low wail of the sirens creeps into the church. It seems muffled, as if it hadn't been invited in.

You fall asleep.

There is a creak and you jump.

'Hello?'

The voice of the priest.

'My child, did you want to confess?'

You sit up straight.

'Yes, Father.'

'Go ahead.'

'I committed obscene acts, Father.'

'On yourself or on someone else?'

'On you, Father.'

You smile. You like the silence that follows.

Outside, the sky is turning grey. You hurry. You walk past the plant where women work. You stop to look at them. Their gestures are as perfectly timed as the short hand on the clock in the living room. Fine and exact. Precise, female hands.

They are making weapons. Turning pots into warships.

They wear berets, and their clothes have a sober, military cut.

They are like ballerinas. The elegance of the useful gesture.

They are also a motivation, a reward. The men who go off to the front fight for them: their beauty is part of the war effort.

Way in back, you think you spot Hilda Strike, dressed to run, her slender body and warrior presence. She looks up at you.

It's raining. You walk slowly home.

On the radio in the kitchen: 'At 5:45 a.m., the Operation Neptune fleet opened fire on German defence forces.

'At 6:30 a.m., the first waves of the American assault force landed on Utah and Omaha beaches. In the British and Canadian sector, the attack was launched one hour later because of the different tide times.

'We do not yet know the extent of the losses, but the Atlantic Wall seems to have been breached along its length, and the Allies have penetrated some six miles inland.'

You, your mother and your sisters are standing on chairs, rags in hand. You are washing the windows.

You are astonished by the differences possible between two lives. This morning, a soldier was running through the sea at Normandy, dancing with death, praying to his mother to watch over him.

You look at your mother. She seems so delicate and small. You could take her and crush her. She notices you looking, which makes her squint in irritation. She turns her head, as if you were giving off too much light. She sends you back to your work with a subtle gesture, pointing to the slimy trace of an insect.

A bird flies into the sparkling clean window. It falls to the balcony. You are fascinated. You love surprises. You rush outside. The bird is there, lifeless. You don't dare touch it in front of your mother. You know she would wash you in bleach.

But she bends over the bird and picks it up with a tenderness you have never seen in her before.

She cups her palms and the bird curls up in them, as if it were made for her hands.

You aren't sure who is holding whom. Has the bird picked up your mother or has your mother picked up the bird? For a moment, it is unclear.

They seem fused, like glass sculptures. Frozen in the rift of time where the idea of death stealthily makes itself known. Your sisters don't move. Neither do you. Standing in this strange moment, just before life resumes its course.

Then your mother's voice emerges: 'Suzanne, the garbage.'

She wants to get rid of it, suddenly, right this minute.

You obey. You go get the garbage can inside the house and return, holding it out to her. She tosses the dead bird into it with a brusque gesture, as if parting with a bad memory.

Then she goes back into the house and washes her hands. She scrubs for a long time. You watch her from behind, her neck about to crack.

You imagine her crumpled on the ground. You would have done the same. You would have picked her up, crumb by crumb, held her in the palm of your hands, and quickly tossed her in the garbage.

You tie the bag with a solemn gesture and carry it to the side of the road.

Edmond Robillard did his novitiate with the Dominican Fathers in Saint-Hyacinthe. He offers his services as a spiritual advisor to youth in need of moral guidance.

You go talk to him a few times. Initially out of pressure from your parents, then for pleasure.

The Dominican Fathers live and pray in a large grey building at the corner of your street. You walk by it on your way home from school. You are welcome; you can pass the time there.

You think Hyacinthe, his religious name, is funny. And his turtleneck suits him. You don't tell him, but you can't stop looking at it.

What you like about the turtleneck is imagining what's behind it. His long, straight neck. A few fine, purple veins, delicate, almost graceful.

You know that it bothers Hyacinthe when you stare at his neck, but you like that too.

So you visit him when you walk by, when your heart is light.

He asks you questions. About your worries, your pleasures, always trying to get at what you believe.

He knows you are bright. Your grades at school prove it.

He feels like you are destined for great things, if you can get your wild streak, which he has already sensed in you, under control.

But Hyacinthe understands that holding you back would do you a disservice.

So he suggests that your parents sign you up for a big public speaking competition in Montreal.

He thinks you can do it.

The idea of taking the train, and then the more vivid one of seeing Hilda Strike's city, makes you deeply happy.

Achilles and Claudia agree.

You have never loved them so much.

You are eighteen years old.

You have polished your ankle boots, and you are wearing a boater Claudia has given you for the occasion. Achilles has shaved his beard and put on cologne. He won't tell you he is proud of you, but you know he is.

You say goodbye to him as if you were leaving to go far away for a long time.

You board the train, hanging on to your small suitcase. Your palm is clammy.

You walk down the aisle, glancing at faces as you go. Your eyes leave a mark, but you don't know it yet. Something you got from your father: piercing eyes that leave an impression.

From outside the window, Achilles watches you go. His big girl is such a good speaker and is off to speak in Montreal. You sit down and look at him. He looks like he's going to cry, but he is old enough to have watery eyes, so you're not sure.

The train starts up, and already you're not looking at your father. You are looking ahead.

The scenery rolls by and disappears in the distance. You calmly take in everything. For the first time, you feel like this is where you should be. Where things are moving.

Hours pass but you don't get tired, your body calmed by the forward movement.

Anything is possible now.

You stand, sovereign. And you walk slowly down the aisle of the rocking train. You are rooted, enduring.

You take a look around. As you walk, you come across a man on his own, dozing.

You sit next to him. Your thigh brushes his. You watch him sleep. His head bobs in time with the train. You gently take his jaw and move it toward the hollow of your shoulder, which you offer to him.

He stays there for a while and then surfaces. You bore your eyes into him. You don't need to smile at him. You introduce yourself: 'I'm Suzanne.'

He takes you in all at once, all of you, too much woman on offer to him. He stammers his name, which you don't remember, because you don't care. Finally you smile at him before getting up and moving on to another solitary man.

The Salle du Gesù is full. It surprises you. All these young people spending an evening listening to others speak.

The audience is facing an empty, plainly lit stage, onto which the speakers are already filing.

Each speaker will make a speech, arguing an issue of their choice for ten minutes. What counts is style and rigour.

A tall young man is already standing on the stage. He is wearing a black jacket that makes him look like he has broad shoulders, which he squares before the crowd, his torso on display.

His thighs also seem slightly spread, giving the fleeting impression of a body in freefall. The audience is instinctively attentive, trying to catch him in mid-flight.

The words flow from his mouth, slow and expansive, reaching audience members like smooth, viscous lava from a volcano.

There is no escape.

At the end of his speech, there is a moment of silence before the applause, the bodies stunned by the impact of the encounter.

Leaning against a wall, you are moved. You can't sum up what was said. It was something about systems of thought and worlds to invent.

But the man, with his controlled freefall, has captivated you.

It's your turn. You walk the distance that separates you from the stage, and already you feel like you are foundering a little. You know your speech and you know you can deliver it.

But suddenly the crowd seems alien to you. You don't know if they like you. You haven't had time to make sure.

You climb the three steps and find yourself higher than all of them.

At the back of the room, you see the man who, a few minutes before, controlled his fall so well. He is studying you. Yet his strength has an aura with a clear crack. Which you feed from.

And you dive in. You are talking about the end of the war. Of the freedom it has brought women, who are finally out of the house. You know that this sounds shocking: a woman's place is in the home.

The words are formed round in your chest and grow moist in your mouth. You magnanimously send them out into the room; you offer them up. *Here, come have a taste.*

People are listening to you, at first tentatively.

You spontaneously stop for a moment. Something is missing. You pull out your red lipstick and excuse yourself as you paint your mouth crimson. You get a few laughs, just a few. You accept them. The lipstick is the elegance your words were missing. You change from a girl to a woman, and you pick up where you left off. The workers at your plant become more elegant, their gestures become more graceful, almost mesmerizing. A page of history has just turned. They can be women and factory workers.

Everything about you speaks of a new era. You stand tall, and despite your diaphanous skin, it seems as though you have just invented the world. You talk about possibility, and it is moving that something huge and invisible is growing from such a slight presence.

You finish. You get a standing ovation.

You win the public speaking competition.

The young man of the cleverly controlled fall comes to congratulate you. Even up close, he looks like he is falling. He introduces himself. His name is Claude Gauvreau.

He invites you to spend the evening at his friends' place. Delighted, you accept.

In the living room of a small apartment on Rue de Mentana, a few young people are smoking and talking. Drawings are scattered on the floor.

You immediately want to stay. To make this cloud of smoke, this circle of words, yours.

There are around ten people, mainly boys, but you look at the girls first. There are three of them. They exude elegant simplicity. Claude introduces them. Marcelle Ferron, Françoise Sullivan, and Muriel Guilbault. They glance at you; they don't feign warmth, but they invite you to sit down.

The men are engaged in a lively discussion about the ink drawings strewn on the floor. They don't look like anything you recognize. You could lose yourself in them. You understand that, beyond these walls, they would be considered offensive. You feel privileged to be spending time with the offenders.

What is being discussed seems important, but the drawings are just tossed on the floor as fodder for discussion. You like this disconnect between the idea and the object.

Claude, who seems to come down to the ground in this place, stops falling for a moment and introduces you to his brother, Pierre, and then Jean-Paul Riopelle and Marcel Barbeau. They are all around your age.

Marcel asks about the public speaking competition. Claude shrugs and points at you.

'I lost,' he says.

You know you should smile, but you tend to forget how in this sort of situation. So you just stay in the moment and let a brief silence of acknowledgement settle around you.

Mr. Borduas, who you are told is the host, and who until now has kept to himself, approaches and offers you a glass of wine.

'Congratulations,' he says.

He is about twenty years older than the others. He is short, with a prominent forehead and the sad eyes of the overly intelligent, which are tucked under bushy black eyebrows. You understand right away that he is the leader.

And you want leaders to like you. You watch him. He withdraws, a little removed from the group of young people, where the conversation has resumed. They are discussing Jean-Paul's latest ink drawings. Their explosive subjectivity. You understand nothing, but you could swim in these ideas for the rest of your life. They are exhilarating.

Marcel reticently places a sketch on the floor. It's his turn.

There is a barrage of comments. No one says whether they like it or not. They are trying to get a word in about the abstraction. What is its source? Should it survive?

You think it's incredible. There is a rough sensuality you would happily stretch out in.

Borduas approaches the circle. He glances at Marcel's drawing; Marcel is on the edge of his seat waiting for him to speak. Then he looks at you. You have captured his attention.

You say it's beautiful. That you want to lie down and be swallowed up in it.

Borduas laughs. A spontaneous, subdued laugh. It seems to happen rarely, because at first everyone is shocked, and then they all do the same.

It's midnight, and everyone seems to know it's time to leave.

The wine has brought you all closer together. Marcelle, who is feeling jovial, has taken you under her wing. She gives you a warm hug.

Borduas retreated to his quarters after offering you Marcel's drawing and saying good night. Marcel, curled up like a snail in its shell, hides behind the smoke. You ask him whether he wants you to have his drawing, which you like. He grumbles a hollow yes.

Claude offers to walk you back to the station.

On the platform, in the middle of the night, you agree to write to each other. It will change the course of your life.

On the train back to Ottawa, you feel as though you are the only one moving and that everything else is standing still. The night outside is deep and radiant. You have Marcel's hypnotic drawing tucked in your pocket. You have a geyser in your stomach and there is nothing around you to stop its gushing.

You knew nothing about Montreal. Aside from Hilda Strike and snippets about Duplessis.

You still don't know much more than that. Except that a door has opened onto bodies in motion, bellowing in a cloud of smoke, sipping and sharing wine, reflecting on arcane, appealing shapes.

These people have rekindled your interest in others.

You were an island, and now you feel like you might have a country.

You return home ecstatic. Things go back to normal, but you navigate them differently. Swimming with the current. Now you know that there is somewhere else out there for you.

What you don't know is that there will always be somewhere else, and never the same place. That will be your undoing.

You receive a letter from Claude. He kept his promise. With a friendly, uncompromising pen, he rails against the repressive climate that surrounds him. He rants against the Padlock Law, passed to fight communism, which holds his artistic pursuits in contempt. He seems to enjoy being an agitator.

In a passionate postscript, he encourages you to read Lautréamont's *Les Chants de Maldoror*, Maldoror being the devil's alter ego. Excited by the idea of reading everything ever written by an author banned by Duplessis, Claude has taken him for his hero and proudly admits that he has managed to get his hands on a copy.

He includes a few excerpts for you. It's repulsive and modern. You don't like it. And you tell yourself that you would have banned it too.

All the same, the daring speaks to you. But what wins you over is Claude's mischievous enthusiasm. He is quenching your thirst.

> It was a spring day. Birds spilled out their warbling canticles, and humans, having answered their various calls of duty, were bathing in the sanctity of fatigue. Everything was working out its destiny: trees, planets, sharks. All except the Creator!
>
> He was stretched out on the highway, his clothing torn. His lower lip hung down like a soporific cable. His teeth were unbrushed, and dust clogged the blond waves of his hair. Numbed by torpid drowsiness, crushed against the pebbles, his body was making futile efforts to get up again. His strength had left him, and he lay there weak as an earthworm, impassive as treebark.
>
> [...] A passing man stopped in front of the unappreciated Creator and, to applause from crab-louse and viper, crapped three days upon that august countenance!

You learn that thousands of bodies have been incinerated. That they left on trains, alive, with their families. That they didn't come back.

People are hinting about it behind closed doors. It seems that a fine rain of white ashes fell on neighbouring cities.

The huge gulf that separated you from the horror gets wider in your chest.

Did people get out their umbrellas? Or stick out their curious tongues, letting the metallic taste of the fate of those people settle on them?

For the past few days, people have been singing and hugging in the streets. The war is over. Mothers are being reunited with their sons and women with their lovers.

At first, you applied yourself when you wrote to him. You polished your syntax and narrative. You wanted him to know that it mattered.

Then, inspired by his writing, you slowly let loose. Strange words started coming together, ideas melting into one another and becoming blurred, even your penmanship grew untamed.

He read your letters and enjoyed them. An invisible drawbridge now connected you.

May 10, 1945

Dear Claude,

    Your letter was such a treat, torrential and mad.

    You inspire me to take risks and I plunge.

    My cold hand like an earthquake.

    Torment contained.

    The victories stillborn in the gloom hum an uncontrollable smile.

    A finger trembles on the verge.

    I want to touch the wound like a down cushion.

    Here is the back of my hand,

    Like a liqueur.

Suzanne

You get a letter from Montreal. Not from Claude, but from Collège Marguerite-Bourgeoys, where you have been accepted. You will study classics.

You know that you will never come home. And you don't hide it. Everything about you is saying goodbye. The way you look at your sisters, and then your brothers, lingering too long. Your half-smile to your motionless mother, who won't meet your eyes, who is constantly trying to hold back tears. Your subtle, awkward gesture to smooth her wrinkled apron rather than hugging her. Then, the coldness you slowly let settle in between you and them. It emanates from you, from an arctic, glacial, brittle source. The ties freeze and crystallize: you find the power inside you to make a clean break.

Your stony eyes bore into those of Achilles, with his tousled hair and scratchy beard. This time, he would like to keep you close by. But he nods his head, a feeble protest against the oppressive stillness of goodbyes. And with a heavy, loving gesture, he points to the door. He is letting you go, with the regret of a fisherman throwing back his best catch. This one was too wild for him.

Steeped in pride, you walk through the door without tripping.

Then, you turn gracefully and head back toward the piano. You play a scale on it, standing, as you and your mother avoid looking at each other one last time. You play a legato scale, holding down the pedal to make it resonate.

Not so much as a challenge. More as an invitation.

1946—1952

There is something about Montreal that is like you. Maybe the language in part. With your love of words, you feel at home here.

Unlike on your side of the river, French is praised and appreciated here. It is celebrated at conferences; societies are founded to defend it, preserve it, purify it …

Your father would be proud to see you immersed in a place where your language is thought of as special.

You explore the city on Claude's arm. He takes you everywhere. He has the long stride of the men who cleared the land. It's as if he is stepping over a river or a ditch with each stride. You do your best to follow him, your arm hooked through his.

He cleaves the air, his head down. He explodes, in torrents, against everything, against everyone, and mostly against himself.

It makes you laugh, but he doesn't notice, he is so consumed by his passionate flights of oratory. When he stops to catch his breath, you step into his line of sight, wanting to remind him you are there. And when you manage to get him to see you, when his focus is finally on you, you don't know what to do with yourself. You look for something to do. You look for something to say. You are intimidated not so much by him, but by this new life of yours, which you still know nothing about. You feel like a child who has bitten off more than she can chew. It excites you and scares you.

You travel the city by streetcar, with no particular destination in mind. Claude is your guide, unwrapping the city for you as he talks, like an endless gift.

You jump from one streetcar to another. You slip between the strange bodies. You wrap yourself in their nameless presence. You lean against the travellers, pressing your neck or the curve of your back against a shoulder or a hip.

You like feeling the weight of other people on you. You leave your imprint on them. Leave it on stranger after stranger. It's your way of making your mark on the new landscape.

You get off the streetcar at random, go into a stationery store and try all the pencils by writing verses in four hands, take a detour down an alley where time stands still while a withered woman slowly trims her eggplant blossoms with the care of a lacemaker, then you climb up to the roofs to see the city into night, sharing a Du Maurier between you.

One evening, Claude takes you to La Hutte, a little bar downtown. His friends are waiting there for him.

You are nervous about being in front of all these strangers. You feel as though you are trailing sludge behind you. As if everything about you has nothing to say.

La Hutte is a warm place. You are reassured as you walk in. Long tables are lined up, with groups of young people sitting at them, sharing a single warm beer that makes the rounds for hours.

It's a place for poor people to enjoy themselves. A place where they are left alone. You are entitled to be there.

You hide behind Claude, who is striding across oceans to reach the table.

You are surrounded by beautiful faces. Some of them are familiar.

Abandoning you to your fate, Claude sits beside Muriel, whom you recognize from Borduas's studio. You feel lost. You hesitate between doing an about-face and taking off your sweater to flash your breasts.

Marcelle turns toward you, and, with an animated gesture, invites you to sit down. The beer has landed in front of you, and she offers you a sip.

'Hurry, before it gets passed on!'

You sit down. Your legs are nice and warm under the table. Marcelle's slender, fidgety body is a counterpoint to yours. And, slowly, you put down roots.

There is a bluish sandwich in the centre of the table. In a stream of words that collide between Marcelle's thin lips, she explains that it's a Duplessis sandwich.

You have to eat to drink here. So the same baloney sandwich on white bread has been sitting as a foil in the middle of the table. For days, maybe weeks. It's become the bar mascot.

Marcelle makes your head spin with happy chatter that warms you and that, gently, helps you settle in.

Marcel is across from you, still brooding. He is not looking at you. He is concentrating on the serious arguments being made by Jean-Paul, who is tall, reaching to the sky, with an angular face and dark eyes that seem to be looking beyond the walls.

Marcelle elbows you, amused.

'So, which one do you want?' she asks, looking mischievous.

You like this girl already.

'I can't decide ...' you answer, smiling.

You look at Claude, who is sitting at the end of the table. Beside him is Muriel, red-haired and wild. Claude is animated and suave and is devouring her with his eyes.

'Forget him,' Marcelle laughs.

You can't help but notice the round, enticing breasts Claude is taking in.

Muriel is an actress. She is Claude's raw material. When she is near him, she stops his fall. Without her, he is always off kilter.

Being all woman, you have a hard time resigning yourself to this shadow cast on you. But it is created by a blazing sun, so there is nothing you can do about it.

Marcelle asks you what you do. Where you're from. She looks perpetually amused, has short, messy hair and keeps shuffling her feet under the table like a nervous child. You trust her. Is it because she smiles at you or because she is not threatening to you? Either way, you want to be her friend.

You tell her you're from Ottawa. That you are ... a student. And that you write, sometimes. Your face gets hot.

Marcelle is delighted with your answer. An Ontario poet. She thinks it's exotic.

She raises the only glass on the table in the direction of the Swiss manager and shouts to her, 'Our glass is empty. Fill 'er up. It's my round! To the little Ontario girl's health!'

The evening goes on. Censorship is put on trial for the umpteenth time, without anything new being said. They are content to criticize, and they do so enthusiastically.

You don't dare admit that you would have banned Maldoror too.

Jean-Paul and Claude get angry, two cocks fighting, forgetting the reason, contenting themselves with snatching words and detonating them.

They are handsome and proud. Their rhetoric is rich and profound. You are lightheaded and feel a touch of pride. You belong at this table.

You turn toward Marcel, who is still silent.

You tell him that you still have his drawing. He holds your gaze for a moment, and his eyes trail down your cheeks, over the outline of your lips, landing safely in the hollow of your neck.

Marcel has a solid presence. Grounded. Nothing ephemeral. He is firmly rooted, yet remains elusive, deeply secretive.

He is slender and moves with grace. He would like to be a shadow, but captures the light despite himself; it sprawls lazily over his angular body.

Behind his pale skin, there is a gulf of tenderness.

Marcel is a creature in glass.

A November night, sharp and taut. A night so cold that movement becomes syncopated and slowed down.

You abandon yourself to it with pleasure, following Marcel and Jean-Paul, who have invited you to join them on a mission in the port.

Energized by your presence, the two young men initiate you to their nighttime rituals.

You have to become invisible. Something you're not particularly good at. You welcome the challenge.

The metallic glint of the river, the looming silhouette of boats at rest, the quiet sound of the water, all create a humid, dream-like scene in which you blend perfectly. You tiptoe so as not to disturb the essence of the place.

Marcel and Jean-Paul have a mission. They have come to get tarps, the ones that cover cars that have just been unloaded on the docks. They have done it before. They walk toward a large ship, waiting to be loaded. With smooth gestures, slowed down by the cold, they rip the jute blankets from the cars, wrapping them around themselves.

They cover themselves in them. Every possible surface of their bodies helps transport the precious cargo.

A roll around the neck, four under the arms, they become strange miscreants, eight-legged aquatic creatures, propelled by their grand plans.

You grab as many rolls as you can.

A dog barks in the distance.

Your new friends, transformed into outlandish beasts, surreptitiously stop their synchronized movements.

Then they get back to work. You end up fleeing through the metal cargo, in the belly of a glacial night, a dance you will become accustomed to.

Because you will create your first paintings on these jute canvases.

The dawn light blankets the city. It revives Marcel, who opens up and unfolds. Looking you almost in the eye, he asks if you would like to join them at the studio for a nightcap.

The stairs creak. On the second floor of a small apartment, a garret. The space is minuscule, the ceilings high. Frost forms on the walls; the outside light shines through it.

There are jute rolls everywhere, and you add the ones you are carrying to the pile. Painted canvases are pinned to the walls, like exclamation points, in stark contrast with the calm of the new day.

Jean-Paul gets a fire started in the small, rusted potbelly stove, which sits proudly in the middle of the space. You notice three painted circles on the floor.

He explains that the first one, the red one around the stove, designates the hot zone. The second, the green one, the temperate zone, and the third, the blue one, the cold region.

And that it is best to paint in the temperate zone, unless one is going for high drama.

Marcel, still bundled up, his head in a wool hat and leather gloves on his hands, serves wine in metal cups. The wine warms you a little. You sit in the hot zone of the small studio and shiver. Jean-Paul passes you a jute tarp, which you roll up in. The kindling slowly catches.

Jean-Paul has been sharing the studio in the alley with Marcel for a few months now. He used to paint at home, until his family burned all of his work, which they deemed subversive. All that was left was half-charred wooden frames.

Marcel takes out a can of paint, which he opens. It's enamel.

'This is what nice cars are painted with,' he says, with a first, faint smile.

He dips a brush in, and then he starts to spatter colour in front of him on a canvas hung on the wall, with sharp, arrow-like gestures. He dances, and red rain explodes on the former cover of a car in transit.

'This is how he warms up,' Jean-Paul whispers, throwing a big log on the fire.

You finish your wine in silence. The day drifts gently toward you, sliding across the stained old wood that you are pleased to be sitting on.

It's the beginning of your first winter in Quebec.

Jean-Paul is snoring at your side.

Every afternoon, after his day at the School of Furniture, Marcel works with his Uncle Georges at the butcher's. He cuts up poultry and pieces of meat. He likes this physical work and sees parallels between how he earns his living and intense moments of creation. His hands in the red flesh, he strikes blows with the knife, cutting at just the right place, slashing what was formerly alive to give it a new shape, one of his own making. He doesn't overthink it and moves instinctively.

In these hard times, his knife slices through older animals, brought to the butcher's by their starving masters.

This is what happened to Octave. A horse. Not purebred, but a good horse. Octave was an outstanding workhorse, earning him a great deal of affection from his masters, who were good Christians. Which is to say they had twelve children conceived out of duty, without looking each other too much in the eyes, children who now enjoy counting angels and multiplying prayers in math class, as prescribed.

The picture of Maurice Duplessis was the first thing Madame Pion, Octave the horse's mistress, would dust upon rising.

She always offered him a submissive smile, tinged with desire. He was the love of her life.

Obviously, the Pion family was upset when Maurice lost power in 1939 and had to relinquish his position to Adélard Godbout's Liberals.

But Maurice's portrait never relinquished its place in the living room, and the Pions continued to live in awkward denial, taking pleasure in thinking that their king still reigned and Quebec was on firm footing.

When a small Duplessist delegation came to visit the Pion family, one cold morning in the winter of 1943, Octave was bent over his feed, enjoying his breakfast.

Steam was coming out of his nostrils; a fine frost had formed on the tips of his ears. He felt good.

The three men stopped in front of him to eye him up and down, before going in to have tea in the Pion living room. Looking official in their ties, they confirmed to the Pions that they wanted Duplessis re-elected. Monsieur Pion searched for the right words to show his support. Madame Pion fluttered about, trying to find a few things to set on the table.

The three men were serious in their role as investigators, smiles calculated and gestures precise.

Then, reassured, they got up to leave. And, in the doorway, the tallest one asked Madame Pion if she had lost any children. Madame Pion froze.

'Yes.'

The man asked for their names.

Madame Pion mumbled the names of the three children she had lost. The man noted them, barely hiding his satisfaction.

Then came a final question: the old horse outside. Does it have a name?

This time, Monsieur Pion answered.

His name is Octave. He's not that old.

The man noted the horse's name. On the same line as those of the children. Then, politely, the delegation slipped away. Octave watched them as they retreated into winter.

On August 30, 1944, Maurice Duplessis was re-elected.

Unfortunately, Madame Pion had refused to exercise her newfound right to vote, because her place, and she truly believed it, was in the home.

Plus, Maurice had told her that the women's right to vote is unconstitutional, since the Constitutional Act of 1791 stipulates that only 'persons' can vote and that the term 'person' applies only to men.

People now say that the names of dead and buried children helped carry Maurice Duplessis to victory, artificially swelling the ranks of voters.

We know from a reliable source that the list of electors included the name of Octave Pion. Workhorse by trade.

Years later, having grown thin and useless, he was taken to the slaughterhouse, where his previously valiant body was cut up, then sent to the Boucherie Saint-Antoine, where, on that particular afternoon, young Marcel is working at a furious pace.

He has to wrap up the pieces of an entire horse for a priest who is having company for dinner and then leave on time for the premiere of *Bien-être*. The entire group has spent months working on the play written by Claude, and that evening will be the first performance. Marcel has to help put the set together, and he is worried sick he won't get there on time.

You are waiting for Claude in the small room you rent. The walls around you are bare: you deny yourself any decor. You enjoy things in motion. So your suitcase is still open, your clothes folded inside, the drawers empty.

Claude comes to pick you up in the afternoon. You are going to help him set up the theatre.

On the way, you stop to pick up Marcel, his hands still bloody. It's his set, his creation. It can't be put together without him.

Claude steps behind the counter. Marcel is wrapping large pieces of meat in newspaper. Easy enough. Claude imitates him to speed things up. You join them.

First with your fingertips, starting with small pieces, which you gently wrap in the used paper.

Claude is working with broad gestures, very much like him. He starts reading from the paper he is using to wrap a large thigh: 'Whether one thousand years ago or today, the Church is the only thing that will save the world!'

You smile, finish rolling a filet and grab the offal Marcel holds out to you.

'Christianity can address the problems of any age: it is the only doctrine for man because it meets all of his needs and takes into account all of his weaknesses.'

You grab a page from the paper and put the animal's soft, warm heart on it. You like touching the meat with your hand. You can sense the life that was once there. You squeeze your fist around the heart before wrapping it up.

Claude roars now, still reading from bloody pages: 'Most importantly, Catholics, who are fortunate enough to know the truth, have the solemn duty to spread it.'

Marcel laughs. He has a broad smile, with fine, well-shaped teeth. And his laugh is brittle. Rare and precious.

Octave is wrapped in pieces. The priest comes in, looking jovial. He is a regular customer and greets Marcel like he knows him. Marcel hands him the butchered animal, wishing him *bon appétit*.

Your hands are sticky. Claude asks you whether you want to read an article that is perfect for you, entitled 'Ladies, your home is your empire.'

You say no: it's time to go. Marcel closes up the shop, leaving behind Octave's blood and the words of *L'Action catholique*, required reading for his mother, written by Duplessis's industrious secretaries.

Awakening artistic sensibility is more important than technical training.

Jean-Marie Gauvreau,
Director of the École du Meuble de Montréal

Borduas eats in his office, as he often does. With a sandwich made by his wife in hand, he paces while looking over his students' drawings in gouache, ink, and charcoal.

He occasionally stops for a moment to consider the intensity of an effort, the restraint of another. He notes what needs to be improved. He chooses words that provide the catalyst without dictating the direction. Sometimes he is moved. When that happens, he picks up the drawing, brings it closer to him, meets it halfway.

But today, he is leaving school earlier than usual. He has to go to his students' show. He helped them come up with the set and make the costumes. He thinks the play, written by Claude, is ambitious.

He always locks the door. Out of respect for his students' work. Convinced that he is leaving promising pieces behind him.

In the hallway, he is waylaid by the school's director.

He asks him to come to his office. Borduas explains that he doesn't have much time. But Jean-Marie insists: it's important.

Borduas sits down, annoyed.

Jean-Marie appreciates Borduas and recognizes his talent. But teachers keep complaining that when they inherit his students, it's as if they haven't learned any of the basic techniques.

Borduas has heard it all before. He regularly gets wind of the supposed failings of his courses.

He stays calm; his teaching is oriented toward the individual, the creative process. His colleagues' teaching is oriented toward the end product, the object to be manufactured. The two approaches should complement each other.

Jean-Marie seems sorry.

'This is the School of Furniture.'

Paul-Émile replies, caustically, 'We do drawing, decor, design – more than just furnishings. Many students want to get away from the world of geometry, which is in opposition to the spontaneity and generosity of the creative act, but … '

Borduas is interrupted by his superior: the decision to break with technique has people talking and hurts the school's reputation. His teaching hours will be cut.

Borduas curtly thanks the director and slips out. He doesn't want to be late for the show.

The play is being staged at the Congress Hall on Boulevard Dorchester. You iron costumes while Marcel finishes putting together the set.

Claude is nervous, crouched in a corner, muttering his lines.

Muriel, who is used to the stage, does a few vocal exercises. You like watching her. She is an open window, a choir, fireworks. You, who are more remote and secretive, magnetic from deep within, you envy her burning presence, giving everything she has.

The play puts her onstage, dressed all in white. In it, she marries Claude.

The house is almost full. The lights slowly come down, carefully filtered by Marcelle.

The set rocks when Claude makes his explosive entrance, harnessing the power of the perpetual fall, giving himself completely to the audience, his entire body asking them to open their arms and catch him.

You are sitting in the fifth row, beside Borduas.

Muriel joins Claude onstage; she is radiant in her modest dress.

Claude spouts his lines like a hymn, savouring each word, aware of their fragility: 'Hands in the abyss making leaves. That's a wedding. The cup running over with love like seaweed on the steps. A stream of clouds dives into the hearts: king-fisher. Wreaths in cheeks, peace sculpted in the worried profiles of existence. Sugar woman.'

And at that point, there is a burst of laughter. Quickly followed by more, as if, suddenly, permission has been granted to ruin everything.

Thrown off, Claude puffs out his chest and squares his body, battle ready. He raises his voice, reciting his lines. Muriel looks at him encouragingly, supporting his monologue with her fiery presence, warming his fall.

'Woman with chocolate nails, with eyelashes of armistice, you are mine. I am the seal that has plunged into the streams of syrup. Beaten unfeeling chopped like the notes of a flute.'

Gradually the audience walks out. The house is emptying out. They leave with the scraps of a story, bits of lacerated text. They criticize the form, which is new to them and which they don't understand. This uncertain attempt to liberate the language. Madness scares them. They need signposts. Heading into new creative territory and moving brazenly beyond the boundaries established by academics is a form of puerile indecency with no artistic merit.

There are only about ten people left. Claude and Muriel keep going partly for them, mostly out of pride.

You watch them falling in unison. You spot Marcel in the shadow of his sets. Looking out at the emptiness.

You turn to look at Borduas. He hasn't left. He is listening, his head tilted slightly. There is a softness about him, which you find unlike him. He seems to be receiving the moment whole, floating in Claude's words, in the pair's quiet strength, in the shadows supporting him and in the emptiness gradually gaining on the room.

He feels you looking at him and he turns. His eyes are watering, the glare of a spotlight drowning in them. He is calm. The calm of a person who has just made a choice.

The final words are sent out into the empty room, and the actors leave the stage as one would leave a battlefield.

Borduas stands and applauds.

You do the same.

The past is our master.

Father Groulx

We have to stop the assassination of the present and the future with unrelenting blows from the past.

Paul-Émile Borduas

You order two large beers. Claude looks gloomy. He came crashing down onto the floor of an empty room. No one caught his words, no one interrupted his fall.

Muriel is talking too much and too fast. It's her form of resistance.

Her big eyes have receded into her head. Around them there is just her body, which continues to make gestures, unhinged.

Marcel tells her to be quiet, but she doesn't hear him. Jean-Paul grabs the actress's long hands in mid-flight and presses them to the table. He calmly tells her again to be quiet.

You down half your glass, practically in one gulp, and pass it to Marcel, who seems to have trailed the shadow with him and is now curled up in it.

The door opens, letting in a bit of a storm, followed by Borduas. He hardly ever comes here. He joins you.

He looks at everyone, taking in each person. He looks at you too. He talks to you too. To you.

He thanks Claude for his words. They may not have been good, but they were vivid. Disruptive, refreshing.

He orders seven beers, which are quickly handed around.

He tells you all you are right. Taking risks is what makes you grow. You can't create with an intention in mind.

He takes two big swigs. You do the same.

That you can't plot out the effect you want.

You want him to notice you. Even better: you want to possess him.

Borduas talks without looking at anyone but addressing each one of you directly. He tells you that making sure a work will get a good reception by conforming to established aesthetic norms is an act of cowardice. And that therefore tonight was an act of courage.

You don't feel courageous. But being one of the ones he is looking at gives you strength.

You down the cold beer in one, staring at Borduas, who is wonderfully talkative. The foam runs down your throat, over your tongue, flooding it with bitter bubbles.

He is beautiful when he talks. He gets bigger, as if his body is stretching along with his ideas.

And in his silence, he grows small again, and naked. That's when you would like to grab him and swallow him.

You are a little drunk, which gives you permission. Under the table, you press your thigh against his.

You mumble into your glass, for your ears only, but still at him.

'*Wine with fever goblet. Here I am, harquebus raised on the wire, like lace.*'

You raise your voice, in an easy, amused flow of words.

'*Here is the breath!*'

You grow bold. You plunge. Across from you, Claude catches you.

'*A man on the verge of dance. A condemned man with chains of sun. An elf with the mouth of the moon.*'

Beside you, Marcelle, giggling with pleasure, encourages you to go on.

Your eyes hold those of Borduas, which have come alive, and will not let them go. Your voice is soft and precise.

'*I dance like the mad, joyful muslin acrobatics. Arms, legs, neck reaching for high hopes.*'

Borduas responds, supports you; under the table he presses his body against yours.

Then Marcelle applauds, bursting into joyful laughter.

Someone else carries on. They dive into the words, bandying them back and forth, dirty and raw, volatile and mutilated. You swallow them and spit them back out. You send them up into the air, you wind them in coils, caress them and violate them.

Borduas orders again and drinks to all of you. He wants something wild to grow within you. He puts his hand on your thigh.

Marcel looks at you, and you know he thinks you are pretty. Finally, you are the queen.

Borduas raises his glass to glorious anarchy. It will force us to take our fate in hand.

The owner comes to tell you to quiet down. You're crossing the line.

Borduas goes home to his family, but the rest of you keep the evening going, crowding into the studio.

The jute canvases cover the floor. Some are painting on them, others are writing on them. The place is cramped, and the warmth is welcome tonight.

You fall asleep, drifting off on a drone that is now familiar and reassuring to you.

When you wake up it is light. There are colours around you. It is like waking up in a fall forest with a strong wind. Only the swish of a paintbrush and the breath of a man inhabit the space, which, suddenly, seems immense.

There are ten freshly painted pieces around Marcel, who is still kneeling. He is absorbed by his movements, engrossed in the new piece. Muted sounds intersperse with the sweep of his brush. Guttural sounds, coming from a long way off, from his very own forest, where he likes to lose himself. Still half-asleep, you enjoy watching this willowy animal of a man, his hair tousled and his hand light. He is like a bird. There is something infinitely vast and tender in him, which you notice for the first time.

You close your eyes, leaving him to this flight, because you suspect it is important.

This time it's Claude's voice that wakes you. He is standing beside you, in pyjamas, boots still on his feet. He is holding a steaming coffee pot in his hands. He is amazed by what he sees. The painted pieces of canvas are now hung on the walls, and Claude is pacing the cramped space, taking in each one, impressed by the spontaneous movement. He has never seen anything like it. Marcel is calm, his features relaxed; he has enjoyed the ride. He is smiling, looking at you. He says he has never painted with such unadulterated joy.

You point to one that you find particularly moving. You say you didn't know that an explosion could be reassuring, and yet that is what that painting makes you feel. Marcel mumbles that it's sort of how you make him feel. He isn't looking at you – it's too much for him – but he knows that his words have landed.

The three of you sit down in the temperate zone drawn around the stove and share a cup of coffee.

Automatism was never figurative. Its world is the inner world. An outward projection of the inner world. Surrealism is based on a representation of the inner world, automatism on a non-representation of the inner world.

Claude Gauvreau

You spend the morning at the Tranquille bookstore. It opens early, and they don't mind people hanging around, drifting book to book, page to page. Henri Tranquille is almost always in his office where his correspondence piles up. He is keeping up ties with France and England, to avoid losing touch with what is being written there. To preserve the cracks, allowing words to slip through in spite of the bans.

Tranquille has Sade, Rimbaud, Hugo, Lamartine, Voltaire, and Balzac stashed under his desk. Even Lautréamont. All put on the Index by the clergy, some for heresy or immorality, others for sexual licence or subversive political theories.

Henri Tranquille has read every book in his store, and he can discuss them.

You like touching the books, feeling the paper nip your fingertips. You gather words like nectar, going author to author. When the coast is clear, you approach Mr. Tranquille, and he slips his hand under his chair, ceremoniously offering you a banned copy to look at in the store.

That day, in a corner, Marcel, Claude, and you are quietly reading passages of Balzac. Henri keeps watch, glancing occasionally at the door, accustomed to the risk he enjoys taking.

You would like your words to singe the page too. You would like to have a book that lives on a shelf, somewhere, with your name on it, a book that is alive enough to upset people. Marcel tells you that you should publish your poems. Claude agrees.

'You should publish your poems, Suzanne.'

Duel.

Claude: 'The beggars of Ginglan have stabulary stomatas. On threadbare, concave Duzéates the slight bit of ponterbury proclaims the strapping castucla.

Suzanne: 'The catastrophic gaze of miroben destiny. Road of eripoles! Goodbye, crocophiles, sampolucas, mirconsoles. Goodbye, swollen carlipods, jagged tumours, stained varnish.

Suzanne Meloche was the first woman to engage in automatist writing, similar to that of Gauvreau.

François-Marc Gagnon,
Chroniques du movement automatiste

Marcel has laid a tablecloth on the floor. You are sharing cured sausage and a glass of wine. Steps echo in the staircase. Claude opens the door. He is excited and apologizes for not having been able to resist. He is with Borduas. He wanted him to see.

Marcel gets up, timidly greets his professor, who is wrapped in a long scarf. You get up too. Borduas glances at you without saying hello. He already has his eyes glued to the paintings on the wall. Marcel asks if he can take his coat. Borduas doesn't answer. He is looking at the paintings. His tensed body relaxes like a bullfighter trying to soothe the beast. He steps in to a painting, takes it in his hands, pulls it toward him. Meets it halfway.

'This is shit.'

Then in a professional tone, trying to make up for his remark, he adds, 'It should be an object on a background that extends to infinity.'

Finally, Borduas looks at his student. You can see from the teacher's eyes that he is shaken. You are sure that Borduas doesn't mean what he is saying. And that he is afraid of the man he is looking at. Like a father realizing that his child has grown up too fast.

Claude tries to step in, says in an offhand way that Borduas is trying to impose a form and that that's unfair.

But Marcel tells him to keep quiet.

Borduas scans the walls of paintings one last time, troubled. He is getting ready to leave, stops abruptly in front of a small square of jute cut out and pinned to the wooden wall. You scratched a few words on it before falling asleep.

He turns surreptitiously toward you, stares at you for a thousandth of a second, and then leaves.

Light with the infiltrated prism under the virulent moon.
Ruby seals bloom on my lip like a thundering spark.
A wisp of loving vein on the tongue.

The door is barely closed, the echo of Borduas's steps still resonating in the space, when Marcel grabs a brush and dunks it furiously in the thick, white enamel. The placid white becomes a warrior. It spits on the barely dried canvases. Claude holds Marcel back, begs him not to do it. But nothing can stop his thundering flight, and Marcel gradually obliterates his inspired autumns, lost forever.

Claude leaves the studio defeated.

You undress and stand in front of the passionate work. You stand naked and straight in front of this piece that moves you, your recently awakened skin a shield.

'Paint me.'

Marcel receives you completely. He doesn't shrink from what you're asking. His arm stretches toward the ceiling, frozen in this piece of eternity your body is offering him.

Then, gently, he trails the brush over your breast, down to your hip. It's warm and creamy. His eyes follow the slow movement and the shiver of the paintbrush as it touches your body. He is trembling.

He puts his paintbrush down and continues his slow caress, colonizing your skin with his long, feminine hands.

You slide your hands over his stomach, gently at first, reading it like a rare book. Then you settle in, you press your body against anything you can absorb. With your arms, your stomach, your loins, and your mouth, you wrap yourself around this broken man, this brilliant bird that you make yours, surrounded by the pained white of the obliterated canvases.

You make love under the *Tumulte à la mâchoire crispée*, a magnificent survivor.

It's almost the end of the year, and Marcel isn't painting anymore. A diligent student, he submits his thesis project, earning him his diploma as a cabinetmaker.

Gentlemen,
Here is my thesis project: a house for a painter. It can accommodate four people. A couple and two children.
1st Living room
2nd Dining room
3rd Chairs for the patio
4th Kitchen (standard plan)
5th Bedrooms
6th Studio
The furniture is simple and functional.

Marcel has disengaged, and his wounds aren't healing. At the School of Furniture, the warmth between him and Borduas has returned. As if nothing ever happened. But Marcel won't paint, turning to sculpture instead. He makes his first sculptures, slashing wood and kneading clay. His desire to put his hands on things comes from you.

Marcel no longer paints, except at night, on your body. In the overheated studio, he tames you with drawn-out, opaque gestures.

The two of you inhabit the studio's hot zone, where he skims and teases, spreading the colour over your burning skin. His hand trembles as soon as it approaches you. He forgets his pain, his pride seeping into the surface of your flesh. You make it fragile and volatile.

The night his hand stops trembling, when the brush lands on your skin without a tremor, you ask him to move in with you.

On June 7, 1948, you marry Marcel Barbeau in the parish of Saint-Philippe. You are twenty-two and you become Suzanne Barbeau.

It is raining that day, and you show up at the ceremony wet. Only your witnesses have been invited: Georges, Marcel's uncle the butcher, and Claude, who is disgusted to be setting foot in a church. You have to beg him to be your witness. He arrives wearing a tie, a copy of Lautréamont tucked under his arm, which he doesn't put down once during the ceremony.

The smell of wood and mothballs moves you. The sound of your union bounces off the high ceiling. You suck in your stomach in your little mauve dress. You want to look beautiful. You want to be worthy of this moment.

The priest's deep voice has its place in your story. '*On the seventh of June, nineteen forty-eight, the dispensation of the publication of the three marriage banns having been granted by the ordinary of the Archdiocese of Montreal between Marcel Barbeau, adult son of the deceased Philippe Barbeau and of Éliza Saint-Antoine; and Suzanne Meloche, adult daughter of Achilles Meloche and Claudia Hudon, not having found any reason why they should not be wed, we the undersigned have received their mutual consent and have given them the nuptial blessing in the presence of Georges Saint-Antoine, uncle and witness for the groom, and Claude Gauvreau, friend and witness for the bride.*'

He asks you to kneel. Claude ignores him, making for an uncomfortable moment, which, luckily, the priest doesn't attach much importance to.

Marcel waits until he is outside to kiss you full on the lips. He tastes like white pine, and you want to love him.

A few months later, Marcel gets a job as a cabinetmaker in a small store on Rue Notre-Dame. He makes pretty furniture from rough lumber, and his neck smells like the forest from his long days.

You move to 3195 Rue Evelyn, in Verdun.

You wander along the canal and break up your days with writing. You like writing on the ground. Stretched out or crouching. That way the words can't escape.

In the evening, Marcel comes home, and you make love before you eat. He smells of sawdust and has rough hands.

He wants you to read to him what you write. You do. He likes it.

'Show it to Borduas.'

But no, you're not ready.

The notebooks scribbled dark with words accumulate in your drawers. You want this avalanche to remain yours. At least a while longer.

> *I gather the frenzied sounds at a country pace. I cultivate trembling like pearls. I live candid expectations about to tip. Heavy weight that the crushing freshness of my echo, like a shattering plate. Promising free thought in fragile china. The tablecloth offers me its corner laid out with fruit. I spread my fingers like lace. The brush of the gallop makes me drop my leaves. Caressing depth, so white.*

Marcel takes out a paintbrush. He wants to paint. It's been a long time since he's felt like it. You help him roll out a canvas on the floor. He cuts a small square, the size of a sheet of paper. He wants to illustrate your poem.

That's the day he starts to paint again.

Quebec has become a field of ruins. French Canadians have become a small people whose destiny is decided by others.

Paul-Émile Borduas

At the end of the summer, you are summoned to Borduas's studio. Surprise guests are not allowed.

This clandestine, official appointment pleases you.

When you arrive, hand-in-hand with Marcel, Borduas opens the door himself. Dark circles seem to be propping up his eyes, which are more clouded than usual.

You join the others in the living room. Claude and Muriel are already there; Pierre, Marcelle, and Jean-Paul, too. You all sit, awaiting the others. There is the silence of things brewing, which you don't dare break. Even Claude is quiet.

Borduas is looking out the window. One does not arrive late to such a meeting. A few minutes later, everyone is there. Borduas locks the door and draws the curtains.

He thanks you for coming and hands you a small stack of paper, which he asks you to read. He has waited long enough. He wants to publish, and he wants to do it with you. It hurts him to see you all excluded from the general evolution of thought, and ignorant of important historical facts.

There is pain in his voice. A slight quiver, even, which is not like him. Jitters before a big leap. Casting a shadow over convictions.

You, on the other hand, feel that history is opening up to you like never before in your life. That you are finally leaving behind the muddy shores of your working-class neighbourhood. That Quebec is very much alive. And a work in progress.

Between two verbal outpourings, Borduas seems to choke back the beginnings of a sob. You would like to see him cry. His shell gone.

He turns and tells you to take the time to read his text. And to decide whether you want to sign it. He closes the door behind him and goes out for a walk in the night.

You have only one typed copy between you. There are nineteen of you. Claude offers to read it out loud. But some don't agree and want a first, more intimate contact with the text.

So you get comfortable in the living room. And for three hours, you pass around the pages, in complete silence.

You find the situation both entertaining and disconcerting. You feel like a tightrope walker on the wire of history.

We began to have higher expectations.

[...]

We must abandon the ways of society once and for all and free ourselves from its utilitarian spirit. We must not willingly neglect our spiritual side. We must refuse to turn a blind eye to vice, to scams masquerading as knowledge, as services rendered, as payment due. We must refuse to live out our lives in the only plastic village, a fortified place but easy enough to escape from. We must insist on having our say – do what you will with us, but hear us you must – and refuse fame and privilege (except that of being heard), which are the stigma of evil, indifference and servility. We must refuse to serve, or to be used for, such ends. We must refuse all INTENTION, the harmful weapon of REASON. Down with them both! Back they go!

Make way for magic! Make way for objective enigmas! Make way for love! Make way for what is needed!

We accept full responsibility for the consequences of our total refusal.

[...]

Meanwhile we must work without respite, united in spirit with those who long for a better life, without fear of long delays, regardless of praise or persecution, toward the joyful fulfilment of our fierce desire for freedom.

from *Total Refusal/Refus Global*, 1948

The breathing of the ones who have finished reading joins the rustle of the pages still making the rounds.

Borduas comes into the living room, threading his way quietly, aware of how tense the moment is.

When the last page has been set down, he asks everyone to leave. He wants your answers tomorrow.

He asks you not to talk about what you have just read outside of these walls, and he sees you to the door.

Too inflammatory, too risky. Roger Fauteux, Rémi-Paul Forgues, Yves Lasnier, Madeleine Lalonde, Pierre Mercure, Denis Noiseux, the Viau brothers, faithful friends and close collaborators of the group, refuse to sign.

Madeleine Arbour, Marcel Barbeau, Bruno Cormier, Claude Gauvreau, Pierre Gauvreau, Muriel Guilbault, Marcelle Ferron-Hamelin, Fernand Leduc, Thérèse Leduc, Jean-Paul Mousseau, Maurice Perron, Louise Renaud, Françoise Riopelle, Jean-Paul Riopelle, Françoise Sullivan will sign.

You also agree to sign the *Refus Global*. Because you want to belong, perhaps. Because you want to feel things intensely, like them. To be a true French Canadian. To rebel against your family. To find another family. To break down barriers, like Hilda Strike. That's why you decide to sign.

The next day, the wheels are set in motion. Claude's parents agree to loan you their house to print the manifesto.

You and Marcel manage to unearth an old Gestetner, which you will use to print four hundred copies. Everyone in the group has pitched in, and that's the print run you can afford.

You station yourself near the printer and assist Claude, who operates it. It is slow going. Your fingers are covered with fresh ink.

Borduas has decided to add a few things to the text. A reproduction of one of Marcel's sculptures and another by Jean-Paul. An oil painting by Pierre, and photos of Françoise's dance performances. Three of Claude's plays, including *Bien-être*, will also be added. Other oil paintings, other photos … You do the count. Everyone else has a place on the pages in your hands. Everyone, in one way or another, will be put on the Index. You envy them.

You hand a page to Claude, which he inserts in the machine. It's his poem, which will be the manifesto's cover, along with a watercolour by Jean-Paul.

You ask Marcel to take over for you, handing him the precious manuscript, and you leave the Gauvreau house.

It's already dark out. You run home to get your poems.

It's one in the morning when you ring Borduas's doorbell.

He wasn't asleep. His face is creased and his shirt is open. The wrinkles on his forehead get deeper right before your eyes. You would like to run your fingers over them. Plant flowers in them. But you hold back.

He invites you in. You glide into the hall, confident. He is whispering. His family is asleep.

He looks at you calmly, not surprised to see you. You hold out your poems to him. You ask him to read them. You tell him that you have a place in those pages, too. That you were waiting for this very thing. An invitation like an abyss in which to throw yourself.

He takes the few pages you hold out. He pulls them toward him. He runs his hand over the words without reading them. Pulls a piece of jute canvas from the pile, which he had looked at in the studio. Doesn't read it, seems to recognize it.

His body is close to yours. He has a wild, wounded presence. He smells of warm sweat. He stares at you.

You move closer to him. Your breathing connects.

You ask him whether he will read them. He nods his head almost imperceptibly.

You apologize for having bothered him so late. And you leave.

Claude's mother offers you another round of coffee. The sun has come up. Four hundred copies of *Refus Global* are almost all printed.

Claude is asleep. Marcel has taken over for him at the printer, when Borduas comes to join you.

You try to catch his eye. He strides toward the hundreds of pages that lie on the floor. You have collated them into booklets and are waiting for reinforcements to help assemble them. You have instructions just to fold them, without stitching or stapling, and to slip them in the cardboard cover.

Borduas is nervous. He is pacing the apartment without saying a word.

You approach him. You want to know.

You intercept him as he paces, stepping into his path.

But you are bothering him. You can tell immediately. You are pestering him, and he doesn't like it.

He steps around you and keeps walking, heading toward the window. You realize that will be his answer.

Claude surfaces. His eyes puffy, he helps Jean-Paul fold the booklets. You interrupt them, 'Not yet.'

Claude looks at you, confused.

'We have to start over. I'm not signing.'

Marcel looks at you, stunned. You repeat clearly that you don't want to sign.

Since the agreement was to respect everyone's wishes, no one dares contradict you. Although Marcel tries to reason with you.

'You're going to regret it. And everything is already printed, with your name on it.'

You are calm, but you raise your voice a bit, adding solemnly that you don't think it is well enough written. You think it could be reworked. That's what you think. The text is too dense and complex for a breath of fresh air that should be inviting, light, inspiring. And Borduas's dismissal has hurt you. You want to hurt him back.

He glances at you. You detect a hint of a smile.

He orders Marcel to reprint the last pages four hundred times, without your name.

You leave. It's morning, the stores are opening, families are on the sidewalks. Church bells are ringing.

You wonder whether your river is overflowing and hope that Achilles has new boots.

People around you are talking loudly and laughing. It's a normal, hot summer day.

History has just changed course, and you are standing in the shade.

The *Refus Global* manifesto is launched at the Tranquille bookstore on August 9, 1948.

Your little sister Claire has become a nun. You didn't attend her taking of the habit. You think it's a farce.

But today, you want to see her.

You go to the Sisters of Saint Joseph convent, where she lives now. It is a big, sunny building. Your shoes echo through the empty halls. All of this uninhabited space. Or maybe no space is so inhabited. You feel good here, and that unnerves you. Your religious past clings to you like a second skin.

Claire receives you in the large official sitting room. She sits in an armchair, facing you. You remain standing. Jesus hovers over her.

She smiles. She says you look pretty, that you have put on weight and it suits you.

She congratulates you on your marriage. She is disappointed she wasn't invited. She doesn't say so, but you can tell. She asks whether you are happy. And you realize that is the very question that you came to be asked.

You lie and say yes. Claire knows you're lying.

She asks you whether you have any friends.

No. Not really. You are still a stranger. You have no roots.

You tell your little sister that you're free and that's the way you like it. That unlike her, you like living life on the edge.

You are still standing in front of her as she beams in her stillness.

You shouldn't have come. Claire knows you better than anyone. She can see your chasms no matter what you do.

You have to go. She doesn't stop you.

You leave her a copy of the manifesto, which you snatched in the spur of the moment. The only copy where your signature still appears. Proof of your passage on this page of history.

For a week, negative reviews appear in the newspapers, criticizing both the manifesto and its signatories. Borduas, because of the 'reckless and offensive' remarks it contains, is targeted in particular.

Tuesday evening, you go to his studio as usual.

It's empty.

Claude and Marcel are worried. You know the old wolf is lying low, and you like the idea of him hurt.

You go to his house. His wife opens the door. Behind her, you see his children eating. The mood is gay: bursts of laughter mingled with the pleasure of eating.

'Paul-Émile was fired,' she tells you.

Fired from the School of Furniture, the old wolf.

'He's not seeing anyone right now.'

The beast, decapitated.

It gives you a bit of pleasure. His wife looks at you, overcome. Maybe she spotted the satisfaction in your eyes. Maybe she is wondering how she will survive, with the children and a subversive, unemployed husband.

You gaze fondly at the house one last time. Misfortune has just befallen it and yet it is still cloaked in a raw, landlocked happiness.

You take Marcel's hand as you leave. And you think that maybe one day you would like children.

On October 21, Borduas was relieved of his duties by order number 1394, 'for conduct and written statements incompatible with the duties of professor in a teaching institution in the province of Quebec.'

Marcel finds a small apartment on Rue Jeanne Mance. You live in a double room, which serves as both bedroom and studio. The group drifted apart shortly after the publication of the manifesto and Borduas's retreat, but you aren't bored. You wander along Avenue du Parc to the mountain, which you climb at a leisurely pace.

You come back down through the cemetery. The dead bring you back to your body, acutely alive.

Your step is lighter here. You choose tombstones at random and read the names. Maybe you will find your child's name on one.

You are pregnant.

You go back to the apartment before Marcel comes home, just to lie down a little in the solitude of the end of the day, which is different from the solitude of the morning.

You get the urge to paint.

You unroll a canvas, take out colours and a brush.

You want to paint a bird. A figurative bird, a real bird that is recognizable to the eye and that has no other pretense than to be a bird in flight that people will look at.

So that's what you do. A red bird, with a broad wingspan and a graceful beak. You feel like a woman. Painting without a compass or a ruler. You don't remember this ever happening.

Your bird's flight covers the canvas; you draw a yellow sky for him and wish him a safe journey.

You sign it *Suze, age 22*.

Marcel arrives with his hands as red as a hunter's. Since losing his job, he doesn't smell like sawdust anymore, but he is working hard at the butcher's, and every day he brings home a nice cut of meat, which you share while telling each other about your day.

That evening, you spread the tablecloth underneath your red bird, which is drying on the easel. Marcel smiles, criticizing the conventionalism. Before he starts in on the foundations of the Automatist movement, which you know by heart, you tell him you love him. You list a few names you gathered while walking by the tombstones on the mountain. And you tell him he will be a good father.

You head into town. You have five of Marcel's paintings under your arm, rolled up together. He doesn't want his child to have a butcher as a father. He is an artist, and you will help him.

You walk up Rue Sainte-Catherine to the Museum of Fine Arts. Obviously you know that Borduas and his disciples are feared there, or, at least, unwelcome.

But you aren't afraid. They don't know your face or your name for that matter, because it doesn't appear on the manifesto, the lightning rod of the day.

You stride toward the office of the director. You knock and go in, smiling.

You find him absorbed in something he is reading, which he reluctantly lifts his head from. He looks at you, surprised, and asks how he can help.

You introduce yourself, tell him that you were just popping in, that you know that your being here may seem naive and unorthodox, but that you wanted to show him a few paintings, which you think are splendid and ready to be exhibited.

You know he will either smile or show you the door. He takes a moment to decide, and you take advantage of his hesitation to spread the pieces out before him.

They are part of a highly personal series Marcel recently painted, at night by candlelight. He calls them *Combustions originelles*. And you think they are beautiful.

The director's powers of speech are restored, and he thanks you. He recognizes the signature of the group these paintings come from. He asks you to roll them up immediately. You do so, prepared to leave right away with the paintings under your arm. But at the door, he tells you to leave them. That he will unroll them when the time is right.

You want to throw yourself into his arms, kiss him full on the lips, dance like someone dying of thirst under rain that was a long time coming. But you don't. You leave, barely containing the joy coursing through your body.

You feel like seeing Borduas. To console him, maybe.

You take a detour to his door.

The lights are out. You ring the doorbell. After a moment, you see him behind the glass. He is coming down the long hallway toward you. You notice the way he is walking. Haltingly.

He opens the door. You search for words in the face of his despair. He is absent, hollowed out. You ask him if he needs anything. He doesn't answer. At a loss, looking for a possible spark of joy, you tell him you are expecting a baby. He looks at you then, coming back into his body for a moment.

And then you hear it, behind him. The silence. The black hole created by those who have left.

Borduas is alone. His wife and his children have left. You know he wants to close the door. To wallow in the space left behind. To wolf it down until he vomits it back up.

You take his hand, firmly, and you pull him toward you. You hold him in your arms. Your body is lost. Gliding. You whisper that they will come back. That people don't just leave like that.

When you go home, you find Marcel painting. It is raw and passionate. You are about to tell him that his paintings are sitting in the office of the director of the Museum of Fine Arts, when, beneath the bursts of cyan and magenta, you spot the red wing of your bird. It is all that remains of its short-lived flight.

Marcel tells you that he ran out of canvases, that they have to be used sparingly, that they are scarce commodities.

You ask him to stop for a minute, to interrupt his brushstroke. You approach the painting, and with a childish gesture that you don't explain, you touch what remains of your bird. A few feathers.

You tell yourself that, even hidden, it will survive.

You walk away, leaving him to paint in silence. You say nothing.

You suddenly remember the faint notes of a piano. The spectre of your mother, faded from the years.

There is commotion in the streets. A throng of walkers is protesting the extended imprisonment of Jules Sioui, a Huron. A militant for his people's rights, he has been fighting for years for his nation to be recognized as distinct: they will no longer be forced to go to the front, nor will they pay federal taxes to the colonizer. Jules Sioui founded the Indian Nations of North America before being thrown in jail, where he is in his seventieth day of a hunger strike.

He will probably die. So you march for him. Truth be told, you hadn't heard of him until yesterday. Pierre circulated a letter of support for his cause to the group. A letter you signed.

It's the first trace of you in history. Your signature in support of an 'Indian rebel.'

The bodies meld into one. A warm, fragile stream that takes over the streets of Montreal. Faces meld and feet fall into step. There is a flutter in your stomach. You let yourself be carried by the human current, which rocks you.

The child you are carrying in your belly in the midst of this group of militants is my mother.

Fifty years later, she will dedicate part of her life to Indigenous rights.

It's the moment everyone has been waiting for. The big annual exhibition at the Museum of Fine Arts. In this post–*Refus Global* year, what a lovely surprise to find that two of Marcel's paintings have been selected.

You help him prepare the two pieces. You roll them in thick plastic and tape them up carefully.

Marcel notices how gentle your gestures are. You handle the second painting as if you are swaddling a baby for a nap. You smile at him. He finds you sweet.

You finish wrapping the package and place it on the doorstep, ready to go. Under the plastic, under Marcel's explosive painting, you know that your bird is still flying. It is on its way to the museum.

April 10, 1949. It's your birthday. You are twenty-three years old.

Marcel has plastered the walls of your apartment with his latest pieces.

You enjoy greeting guests at the door. You take their coats; you offer them drinks.

You like playing hostess. You have a round belly, an apartment, a husband who is an artist and friends who have come to wish you happy birthday.

You have a life. You wear it like a thin disguise.

Marcel has brought home meat, again. Claude is barbecuing in the living room. The house smells like grilled fat. The boisterous sound of boozy laughter rings out, and you fall asleep on a pile of coats on your bed.

Marcel is strutting about, decked out in a heavy mask of chain mail he has made.

Tomorrow is the premiere of Françoise Sullivan's dance piece. Marcel spent many nights on the costume, scouring garages and scrap yards to find the materials he needed for the dancer's hair. She will look like she is moving under a heavy claw, trying in vain to dislodge it, with her wild, sweeping movements.

Meanwhile, you're the one struck by a surge from the wild. You have your first contraction. You won't be going to the show.

The wall of your room crumbles in silence as Hilda Strike runs through the celebration.

Your stomach is being torn apart. You crouch underneath your breath, you try to catch on to it again, you look for purchase, moorings; you want to leave your body, but you are holding yourself captive.

Meanwhile, at the theatre, Françoise enters, the lights bathe her, and the metal claw seems to be pulling her offstage. Marcel watches her.

You won't make it, you want it dark, they turn off the lights for you. You look for a hole, earth, a cave.

The door opens, a silhouette approaches on a beam of light. It seems to float. It's Claire. Your little sister. You grab on to her.

She presses her forehead against yours. Puts her arms around your waist. Standing, body to body, you rock back and forth, a slow, rusted metronome. She holds you. You can lift off. Dive in. She tells you to go to that place. So you swallow the contractions. You swallow them whole. For hours, voices mingle with your sweat.

Dawn comes, and the child is born. You hold her warm against you. She smells like moss from the woods. You bury yourself in her. You are survivors.

Claire is gone. You wonder if you dreamed her. The nurses file through, all nuns, all bathed in softness. They show you how to wash your daughter. Your feverish hands find their way. They lather soap on her skin. They direct the stream of the water, sparing a spot on her neck so as not to wash away the smell of damp forest. Your hands quell the burgeoning shivers. They are more alive than ever. They wrap around your daughter, your forest moss, they press her to your body, which is overflowing with sap. Now you have shelter.

Marcel finally arrives at the hospital. He finds you both asleep. You don't see, but he cries a little.

When you wake up, you hold your moss, Mousse, out to him, and he takes her in his arms, trembling.

Everywhere you go, you trail your second dimension with you. You wrap it up in a scarf on your back or your stomach. A direct extension of you.

You go into a church on a winter evening with Mousse under your coat. It's empty and damp. The pews creak in the cold.

You follow the stations of the cross. You know them by heart. But you have a new perspective on them tonight. You stop to study the features: expressions of fear, worry, sorrow, anger.

You are captivated by the story of Christ carrying the cross. You don't want him to die. You catch yourself hoping someone will come and save him. At the thirteenth station, you choke back a sob. Jesus is taken down from the cross and returned to his mother. You whisper, just like when you were ten years old: *We adore you, O Christ, and we praise you. Because by your holy cross, You have redeemed the world.*

Something creaks.

You spin around, afraid someone has heard you.

But the big church is empty.

You head toward the door.

Perhaps to make up for it, you snatch ten votive candles on your way out, which you stuff in your bag.

They will heat the room that is your home.

You drift between the drawings in ink and the photos of performances, your daughter pressed against you.

A few journalists have come out for the occasion at the Tranquille bookstore. It's the first time the group's work is being exhibited since the manifesto was published. You slipped your poems among the pieces. You have nothing to lose. But it's too late, which you realize that day.

You have no status; you are anonymous. You are a satellite to the insurgents. No one is interested in you. You are no one.

You stand tall in this truth, welcoming the critics who deign to introduce themselves to you. You offer them a glass of wine, self-consciously served in the stolen votive candle holders, which the group has carefully cleaned the wax out of. Some people are offended and refuse to drink from them. Others smile uncertainly.

Borduas joins you. You offer him a votive holder of alcohol, proud of this irreverent touch.

He glares at you, a look verging on distaste.

He makes his way quickly through the small exhibition room, glances at the pieces, doesn't say hello to anyone in the group or the guests.

He leaves.

The next day, all the papers can talk about is the infantile insult to the Church, the wine served in hollowed-out votive candle holders. Nothing about the work. Everything about the puerility.

Borduas is furious. None of you are worthy of the ideas you defend. You are still wet behind the ears.

At the same time he tells you that the jury for the next spring salon has decided not to include the Automatist works in their selection.

It's the first time none of the group's paintings will be displayed at this major exhibition.

Sitting at a table at La Hutte, you hold your daughter in one arm and a marker in one hand. Pieces of cardboard are spread on the floor and the tables.

Armed with a stapler, a beaming Claude attaches the panels to each person's clothes.

There is an adolescent frenzy around you. You are glad of it. You need some fun.

The beer and the slogans make their way around the table at the same time: *'Shame on the pathetic jury!' 'We need a jury in step with the times!' 'Let art live!' 'A jury of windbags!'*

You burst out laughing. Mousse is eating chips, surrounded by the wisps of smoke generated by your excited friends. Claude holds her while you slip between two pieces of cardboard.

He cuts a hole right between the words 'art' and 'live.' That way you can carry your daughter, who can slip her head in the middle of your protest.

You are a political woman sandwich, with an activist child as punctuation.

With everyone sandwiched between your messages, you head, full of confidence, to the museum, where the opening for the sixty-seventh spring salon is taking place, filled with habitués.

You go in one by one. You have decided to stay silent. Your adolescent signs are loud enough.

Your arrival interrupts the opening speeches. Two agents head toward you and ask in English, 'What is the meaning of this?' They tell you to leave.

Mousse, strapped to you and already in the shadow of your demands, seems amused as she takes in the scene.

You circle the room twice, meeting the curious looks from the juries and honoured guests.

Some of them recognize you and seem annoyed by the sudden intrusion on their evening, looking down their noses at you. Others seem somewhat amused by the harmless spectacle.

Mousse gradually falls asleep against you, lulled by your silent walk, wrapped in a cardboard demand that is keeping her warm.

The police step in, grab you, and hustle you to the exit.

You all seem small standing in front of the tall museum doors, which are closed again.

Impotent victors. A faint aura of daring surrounds you.

You scatter into the night, each in a different direction. You are children uncertain of their place, refusing to be excluded from their country's cultural heritage.

And you wonder what makes you think you have a place in it.

Your poems lie dormant, shoved deep in your pockets. Mousse drools on your neck. You absorb the lives of others and don't know how to build your own.

There is no one left in the group to envy. Everyone is struggling to survive. Some of them, the ones who can, go home to live with their parents. Others go into exile, in the hopes of getting a chance to paint again, somewhere else.

Everyone is blacklisted virtually everywhere. Banished, undesirable. It's no laughing matter anymore.

Borduas leaves the city and moves to the country, where he finds a little house on the shores of the Richelieu. He gets occasional news from his broken family.

He is shrouded in sadness.

You get an eviction notice. You haven't paid the rent in two months.

The work at the butcher's isn't enough. Marcel's uncle suggests you come live with him. The summer kitchen can function as a bedroom.

But Marcel doesn't want to. He is too proud.

Friends move to Saint-Jean-Baptiste-de-Rouville. They can live on an old farm. The soil is rich for beets, and it will be good for Mousse.

So you gather a few canvases, two or three sheets, some books.

And you head off to grow sugar beets in the country.

This is serious business. Six adults and two young children. All city dwellers, all artists.

You have ten acres of beets to cultivate.

You make an appointment with an agriculturalist. He reassures you: sugar beets are easy to grow.

They are best picked when it's raining. The beets come out of the ground easily and intact.

There is a factory at the edge of the village. Employees come by regularly to get bags by the kilo, and the price is right.

The dirt field reminds you of your mother's ragged nails. You prefer the city to the country.

But your daughter has plenty of people to take care of her, and Marcel is by your side. That makes you happy. You want it to work.

You hoe the earth and start a garden.

Two handsome men, the country in their bones, their step fuelled by the sun, call out to you. They are selling hens. You'll have eggs.

You buy ten and plunge your hands into the soil.

The slender and intense Dyne Mousseau has abandoned her city ambitions as an artist. She has given up being an actress and washes up alongside you on this new continent. She has a daughter too, Catherine, who is growing up alongside yours.

One night, you steal furniture from the village church. A few chairs, a bench you can use as a table.

You sleep on the floor, pressed up against each other. The summer is hot and humid.

Your daughter's skin smells good. You created her. Sometimes when you think about it, you feel stronger than you ever have.

You cultivate your garden to feed her. Soon it is growing.

You drive the tractor to the village to sell vegetables. Mousse clings to you, the little koala. You are getting used to the country. You like being naked under the same T-shirt, and you mend your worn skirts.

You grow proud of the heartiness of your carrots, and you admire the shape of your beans, which you hawk to villagers who know you now.

In the evenings, you collect the scraps of canvas left by Marcel, which you are still writing on. The country has inspired grassroots poetry in you. Fewer flights of lyricism, more bite.

Marcel works all day long in the field. His arms grow round and his face grows angled. In the evening, he eats in silence, and it suits him. He paints on what is left of the canvas, sometimes painting over old ones, the colours accidentally merging.

You make love in the woods because there are so many people in the house. You like it when he is tired. You like draining the remaining life from him, and he likes giving it up to you.

The summer draws to an end over Saint-Jean-Baptiste-de-Rouville, and you are surprised to find yourself quietly content.

The hens haven't laid any eggs. The hens turn out to be roosters. Ten roosters. You've been had.

You break their necks one by one. You cook them down to the bones, which you boil for hours, filling the air in the house that September is settling into.

In the field, beet stems brave the grey, their bright green breaking up the monochrome.

Soon it rains, and everyone heads out to help with the harvest. Ten acres of beets to pull from the ground, in the cold rain.

You plunge your red hands into the mud, eager to feel the bulb of the vegetable, which you loosen before pulling on the leaves, in a clean jerk. The memory of the dandelion fields comes back to you, the rage that you harnessed to pull up thousands of them. You gulp it down. You remember your shamefaced father, defeated, shoulders sagging and heavy. You remember the Hole and the dirty child who may well still be there, stooped and grimy. You remember your fragile mother and her hands tired from rocking her children, the river that unearths the dead and the jam-packed church. You move from furrow to furrow, as in war. You uproot the vegetables that will feed your children.

One day is not enough, and you spend entire weeks outside; you become a field of mud.

Bags of beets are piling up in the house. You sleep with the smell of sweet earth, which turns your stomach now.

Fall creeps between the walls, settles into your bones.

Finally one morning, delivery men from the plant come by. They collect the hundred-odd bags picked by the young people from the city, whom they mock behind their backs.

They weigh them in the back of their truck, and give you a price. You don't haggle. This isn't your world.

You find out later that they paid you half of what they should have for the harvest. No one has the energy to fight. The house is cold. Winter's cruel incursion has started.

You announce to Marcel that you're pregnant.

You take a jar of pickled beets to Borduas, who is still living like a hermit in his little house in Saint-Hilaire.

You tell him about the roosters and the ten acres of beets. It makes him laugh. He seems happy to see you, although he doesn't really show it.

Marcel joins you with Mousse. She is tugging him by the hand, rather than the other way around. He looks lost. A dark, virile silence settles over the two men. It takes up so much space you could touch it. Borduas seeks out Marcel's eyes. Manages to find them. Tells him he will help.

A few days later, you set your suitcase down in a little wooden house, next door to Borduas. Built directly on the ground. Borduas has put up plastic tarps as insulation for the winter.

Mousse shares your mattress. Borduas cuts wood that you take to heat your home.

The next day he finds Marcel a job finishing furniture at Montreal Office Equipment. Marcel leaves early in the morning and comes home late at night.

Your belly grows in the harsh winter. You breathe on the frost on the window and draw three-legged cats with big bums to make Mousse laugh.

You teach her how to use the outhouse. She yells 'Poo!' and you wrap her in a blanket, telling her over and over to hold it in. You whip out into the snow and cross the yard; you open the wooden door with a swift kick, lift your shivering daughter's dress and watch her, full of hope. You shed a tear when she looks at you triumphant, her lips trembling. You are proud of both of you.

You go back in the house, shivering, to warm yourselves by the fire. You boil water, which you share. You tell her stories that you divine in the embers. She listens, entranced, and fights the urge to fall asleep against you.

At the start of the coveted spring salon, Borduas organizes a small exhibition in protest. Everyone who is no longer welcome at the museum, everyone who was overlooked by the noble jurists can, for a few days, foster the illusion that they still exist.

For the occasion, Marcel has painted two large black oil paintings that draw you in. Borduas complimented him, a rare occurrence.

You cord wood orderly and efficiently. Borduas watches you from the window. Your fingers are cracked and frozen. You go into his house to warm up.

He serves you hot coffee.

You soothe your hands on the steaming mug.

He places a stack of papers in front of you, warped with the humidity. You recognize your writing on them. Your poems. You want to tear them from his hands. He senses it.

He pulls out three pages from the pile. He holds them out to you. And tells you that if you still like them, you should exhibit them in Montreal this spring.

— 1 —

Tender farandole under the leaves.
Sweet erosive dance.
Capture cut with the ring on my hand.
Sleep the evening wound.
Silence on the star the eye gives rebirth to.
Dead words like grieving warhead.
Wonderful slaughter to the note sung by a fluted tooth in the mirror.
Floral thrust between the breasts like a damp sponge.
I burn with the fresh secret hollow.

— 2 —

Oh, daunting lake of supreme tenderness, like velvet eyes.
Morning too close to the heart.
Nascent wing taking magnificent flight.
I await the crowns, reward for solitary escapes.
Incandescent halo, standing blackbird with a fluttering song,
Like a stream trickling white columns.
So close to hours of contentment.
Excitement, sensitive grip of my palms between things offered
    up by my dreams.
I finally dip into the sandy water like a spoon in the sun.

I harvest the frenzied sounds at a country pace.
I cultivate trembling like pearls.
I live candid expectations about to tip.
Heavy weight that the crushing freshness of my
echo, like a shattering plate.
Promising free thought in fragile china.
The tablecloth offers me its corner laid out with fruit.
I spread my fingers like lace.
The brush of the gallop makes me drop my leaves.
Caressing depth, so white.

Suzanne Meloche
from *Les Aurores Fulminantes*

The small room is ugly and poorly lit. The pieces have been hung with care, but there are so many of them that they practically overlap.

You are happy to see Marcelle, still just as well put together and talkative. She tells you about her love life and her intrigues. She lays it on thick, and you like it. She tells you your daughter looks like you, and you like it. Claude is there too, with Muriel draped on him like a fur coat. He stands in her light, walks in her footsteps, orbits in her halo. He is happy to see you, and he takes you in his arms and strokes your belly.

Your poems appear alongside his. Your words find each other again, like they did in your adolescence.

The sculpture of a nude towers over them, all length, practically liquid.

The evening goes on, and visitors stream in. You hang back, watching the few curious people who are waiting to read what you've written. Those who make it to the end spend some time looking at the paper, searching for meaning, amused by the bold words.

It makes you smile.

You catch Borduas watching you. Kindly.

It's the first time you feel like you belong.

The door opens and five policemen enter and, with no explanation, take a quick look around the exhibition. They have received reports of an indecent work.

After a brief, decisive consultation, they head toward the naked sculpture and, working in pairs at either end of the undesired body, lift it up and cart it away.

Roussil's statue will spend a few days in jail, under strict orders from Duplessis.

Marcel is invited to show his work in Ottawa. He carefully wraps up his paintings. You don't help him. You want him to stay. Mousse watches him from the corner of the room. He stops for a moment to kiss her. He shuts his suitcase, leaves you a bit of money, kisses his daughter again, asks you not to use the remaining canvases, and leaves.

You hate the void he leaves behind, and you decide to do whatever it takes to ignore it.

That evening, you paint on a huge piece of canvas that you spread out in the kitchen. You paint, your knees on the cold floor and your back hunched. You paint with your claws, foaming at the mouth, your stroke wild. You leave a red scream on the wet canvas.

You fall asleep on it.

Mousse wakes you up, her bare little feet standing on the scarlet canvas, which she looks at, impressed. She has to go. The chamber pot is full. You pick up your daughter, balance her on the sink and roll up the huge canvas. You toss it in the corner.

The pipe is frozen. There is no water. You mash the fresh shit with a fork until it goes down the drain.

The icy morning infiltrates the house. Drops bead and freeze on the ceiling, roll down the windows. Mousse is thirsty: she licks them, drinks them, then huddles up against you, her forehead pressed against yours. Her warm, vaporous breath caresses your face. You close your eyes. Your daughter's tiny fingers roam your cheeks, climb your forehead and get lost in your hair. She tells you a story in her own language, an epic story in which her fingers are the brave explorers of a secret world. You fall asleep, rocked by this new caress, wrapped in your tiny daughter's massive presence.

On May 9, 1951, you give birth to a boy. Black, sharp, intelligent eyes. Marcel is detained in Ottawa where, it seems, 'things are going well for him.'

The wording is ugly and conventional. You don't know what that means, 'things are going well for him.' You know that you are in the hospital, with his son on your chest and his daughter sleeping at your feet. You know the soup they serve you smells acrid. You know that you would like to be able to wash the blood from your thighs while Marcel watches his children.

You know that you do not want to go home alone to your hovel.

You want your man. Your nervous, tormented man. You need his arms around you.

Borduas comes to pick you up at the door of the hospital. He glances at your children, but his eyes don't linger. The sight of children hurts him since his have been gone. He tries his best to deny their existence. He holds the door for you, helps you sit down, and covers you with a coat. Your newborn nestled against your chest, Mousse settled in against you. You would like to drive for days, years.

Your little boy is named François, and he has a soft belly. You put your cheeks on it and rub them over it, then your lips, then your whole face. This body becomes your home, this fragrance your oxygen, all the little crevices – the belly button, dimple, fold – become your refuges, your trenches. You liquefy and spread yourself in a sweet deposit over the warm body of your baby, who lets himself be colonized.

Marcel comes home. You introduce him to François. His son. He takes him in his long hands.

Pride courses through his body, pure, raw joy in the face of a life he has made. He is happy. You prowl around him like a cat, you prod him and smell him.

He grabs you and kisses you. You taste his tongue, which you missed. You melt into him.

Marcel repairs the cupboards, weather-strips the windows, empties the chamber pots.

Then he leaves for New York.

The house is well heated. The children sleep with their hands clenched in fists. You put your hair up, undo a button on your blouse.

You go to them but don't kiss them so as not to wake them.

You leave.

Borduas is waiting for you in the car. He looks at you questioningly. You reassure him. Convince him it will be fine.

You head to the city, to the party. You don't care anymore. You feel like letting loose. Your head leads and the rest of you follows.

The party is in a small apartment downtown. You soak up the smell of cars. You wrap yourself in the sounds, the lights, the movement.

You miss the city life, and it makes you a little dizzy.

You see Claude, Muriel, and Marcelle. Jean-Paul, who has returned from France, and Françoise. Conversations interweave in a smoky living room. Words bore you. You have nothing to say.

You drink and dance into the night. You take your place, relaxed and alone. You don't really like anyone here. You keep to yourself and tire yourself out dancing.

A scream tears through the party.

Muriel has hanged herself in the bathroom.

Claude's fingers search frantically for a pulse, like a divining rod searching for a source.

Muriel is dead. She is twenty-nine.

You help Borduas take the rope from around her neck. You never noticed how long it was. The neck of a swan in flight.

Claude doesn't scream. He doesn't cry, doesn't shake. He is stock still, frozen in horror. He has just lost his ocean. The one that was stopping him from being dashed against the rocks.

The sun is coming up when Borduas brings you home. Your children's steady breathing is a knife in the chest. You run to them while Borduas puts wood in the stove. They are sleeping, huddled against one another.

You get undressed and slip in against them. With a barely perceptible gesture, you invite Borduas to join you. You make room for him. He hesitates. Then he walks softly toward you, not knowing where to put his feet, fearing a chasm, a crevasse, a sudden precipice.

He settles against your cold body, his back to you. His large neck with so many cracks. You hide in it until waking.

Marcel is in the hospital. He melted down in New York. Too much pressure for his fragile shell.

You visit him. He is skin and bone. You would like to fill your hands with his scraps of flesh and wrap them around you like a scarf. He should have stayed with you.

Someone with good intentions left a few newspaper clippings on his bedside table, short paragraphs on an Automatist painter's stay in the American city.

You scan them, throw them out.

You want to know when he is getting out. No one can tell you.

You move in closer to him. You try to draw out his eyes. You blow on the embers. You pull your skirt down to your thighs, take his hand and run it over your sex. His fingers slowly spread in your public hair. Return to their nest. Settle in.

You go back home alone, his imprint on your body.

You are twenty-six today. Rain is coming into the house. The mud from the floor oozes up through the plastic tarps, which have holes in spots.

You buy a pig's leg in the village. You take out a flowered tablecloth that you spread on the kitchen floor. You get the children dressed in their best clothes.

You open a bottle of wine, and you sit there, the three of you. Mousse is almost three years old, her face round like a beaming moon, her eyes gentle. She sits up straight like you have taught her. François will be a year old soon and is stuck to you. If he could, he would melt into you.

You carve thin slices of ham, which you cut into little pieces and hand to them. Mousse is happy to be eating on the floor. She likes picnics.

Your bums are wet, and it makes you laugh.

Mousse sings the song about the snail who sticks its head out when it's raining. Her voice spins out of control, and it's pretty.

You finish the bottle of wine.

You put music on. You dance, François in your arms. Mousse is a minor satellite spinning around you. Their laughter in your wake; you bathe in warm joy and sprinkle it over them.

They collapse on you, asleep, sticky little love leeches.

You put them to bed fully dressed.

You cross over to Borduas's house, where a light is on.

You knock on the door. He opens it. You set foot in his house and decide you will spend the night. You swallow his mouth. You pillage his forsaken body. You water him, you spread yourself on him, you fan out and offer yourself to him, and he finally receives you.

You are twenty-six, and you are parched.

When morning comes, you open your eyes and close them right away. You are where you want to be. You want to go back in time and choose a different path.

It is warm in this man's bed, this older man, his arms like strong roots around your body, which has become a woman's again.

The house smells like paint. What was once the exciting odour of fresh paintings, sudden and still savage newborns. The smell sickens you now.

You drag yourself out of bed. In a small room at the back of the house, they are almost dry. You run a finger along them out of pleasure. The thick, lacquered black collects under your nail.

In the chaotic bounty of the small studio, you spot a copy of the manifesto. Dusty and bloated with mildew, it leaves you cold.

You flip through it at random, riffling the pages between your hands.

Within the foreseeable future, we expect to see people freed from their useless chains and turning, in the unexpected manner that is necessary for spontaneity, to glorious anarchy to make the most of their individual gifts.

Meanwhile we must work without respite, united in spirit with those who long for a better life, without fear of long delays, regardless of praise or persecution, toward the joyful fulfilment of our fierce desire for freedom.

That morning, you could have written that.

As strange as it seemed to you then, now it sticks to your skin.

You go home, and your foot sinks into the floor. It smells like urine and clay. The ceilings seem too low and the walls too close.

The children are awake. François is crying. You wipe his nose on your sleeve.

Mousse is naked, kneeling in the sink. She looks at you hesitantly. You help her.

Shit and black paint merge under your nails.

Then you hear a car. Marcel gets out of it.

You wonder how his feet can touch the ground, his body is so long. You open the door for him, thinking that otherwise he might walk right through it. There is a thin smile on his face. He greets you politely, as if he were walking into his mother's in the middle of the night. You pull a chair out for him. You're afraid he will fall down. He heads toward the children, looks at Mousse, delighted, then François, astonished that he is so big.

A bitter thought hits you. You are that woman. The one who waits, alone.

You have the overwhelming urge to heave. It rises from your stomach, shooting like lightning into your acid throat, which contracts.

You exhale and step outside, just for a minute.

You slip away.

You walk. First with your head bent over the rhythm of your feet. The air stays compressed at the bottom of your chest. Then, slowly, you look up.

You are trying to catch your breath.

You open your mouth. You walk with your mouth open. You cling to the horizon, and you let the air flow in, all the fresh air there is.

When you come back, Marcel is sitting on the steps with the kids. You smile at them, step around them, and go inside.

That evening, you let him go through the unfamiliar ritual. You watch him look for pyjamas, forget to wash faces; they're so happy to see their father. You watch him slip the children under the covers and, with tentative gestures, tuck them in tight, as if he were sculpting clay.

You don't move as you watch the ritual, as if you were at the theatre.

You intentionally withdraw from the scene.

You remove yourself.

That evening, you tell Marcel you're leaving.

You wake up the children before sunrise. Marcel trembles as he makes a black coffee.

Using just your fingertips, you pile the clothes in a little suitcase. You have washed and ironed them. A flowery dress, overalls, tiny white panties. Green pyjamas, yellow pyjamas, blue pyjamas. Diapers.

An organized suitcase.

Before closing it, you put Mousse's little straw hat in it. The one that protects her forehead from the sun. Her prominent little forehead where buds of ideas lie dormant. You will never see them bloom.

She is sitting beside you, watching you. She could ask you why. She could ask you where she is going. But she doesn't. Because she loves you. You turn your back on her, but her eyes bore through you. So you slam the suitcase shut, grab it and leave.

You don't take Mousse's hand. Her palm is a mist-filled chasm you don't want to sink into.

Marcel carries François, and you all leave the family home.

The day outside is lavender.

It's a beautiful day; they had called for rain.

You stand at the roadside. In front of nothing. You are waiting for the bus.

And when you see it coming, you are terrified.

The fake leather of the seat sticks to your bare thighs under your skirt. The bus lurches, and every hole in the dirt road digs your grave. You dry up. You will not cry.

François is asleep. His smooth, rested face, his round, soft cheeks, his raw smell of new flesh, of new sweat. François is a baby. Marcel holds him curled against him. His fine hands dig into the folds of his son's skin. He hides in them for a while, a clandestine immigrant. He wants to lose himself in them and never come back out.

Mousse keeps her head turned toward the window. She watches the scenery roll by, long and flat. The countryside is calming if you breathe it in. She senses danger. She knows without knowing. Mousse is a big girl. Her long, straight neck reassures you. Mousse is strong and has no cracks. Mousse will not falter. Mousse will save her skin, she will wear it as a shield for François, your baby.

The bus slows down. Stops in front of a garage in a little village, where two old people are waiting. They board, excusing themselves. They have the faded presence of existences that leave no clear trace.

They made it through life without making a sound, holding each other's hands. They smiled when they had to. They cried little and never shouted. They sit side by side like they always do. Their smells intermingle, and they think in unison about things that bother no one.

You don't want to die like them. Ordinary.

You finally take Mousse's hand in yours and brand it with the promise of your escape. Hoping that, one day, she will nourish herself from it.

But Mousse is three, and she exists in your skirts and your songs. In the reassuring scent of your neck and the burrow of your arms wrapped around her, she finds her breath.

That morning, on the endless dirt road, you put her heart in a noose; you sever what connects her to the world.

The bus brakes in front of a cornfield. Sainte Marguerite. You're here. You know it, but you don't move.

Mousse stares at you with her jet black eyes. She knows.

'Need to go pee …'

A sentence like a lifeline. A sentence like a lifebuoy you cling to, eyes filled with tears. But you won't cry.

'There's a house over there. Come on.'

Marcel follows you, François still slumbering in his arms.

And you get off the bus that pulls out, filled with ordinary lives, when yours are going to come crashing down in places unknown.

It's a daycare. With lots of toys. The smell of vegetable soup and even a small television, child height.

A mild woman comes out of the kitchen. Her massive husband is in the shadows. A gentle giant. Who eats little girls. But you will never know that.

You head straight for the woman who has agreed to look after your children. Her smile is tender and her apron is flowery. She places a gentle hand on Mousse's round head. Her hands are huge and her nails are painted. She talks to Mousse, but she is looking at you, trying to be reassuring.

'What a lovely big girl you are.'

Gradually, Mousse's hand lets go of yours. You let her slip through your fingers. You lose her.

Mousse moves decisively toward François, now awake, surrounded by cooing babies.

Mousse sits down beside him. She chooses sides. A little warrior.

You scan her territory one last time. Her proud little body, her narrow shoulders, her stubborn eyes that riddle you with bullets of love. The territory that is hers. That you tear yourself away from. Arid, no goodbyes.

You turn your back on Mousse. You turn your back on François. You rush out, Marcel on your heels.

He is crying. He tells you gruffly to stop. That you should both go back. Yes, you should go back and get them.

The wind has picked up. The cornfield bows.

You wait for the bus. Unburdened. Empty. Alone in the gusting wind.

Where is everyone? The sudden breakup of the group was a huge blow.

I'm like a rudderless ship.

You have changed a lot too, Mr. Borduas, changed a great deal. Obviously it's because of the hopes you had and lost. On the rare occasions when I see you, the atmosphere feels strained.

Now I find myself like you. Alone. Suzanne is gone. We left the children where they will be taken care of.

I left Mousse with a heavy heart. I love her.

Afterward, I was so disoriented that I didn't know what I was doing. It all happened so fast. I couldn't support my little family. I lost it.

I still think Suzanne is magnificent, and I love her enough to understand her deep-seated impulses.

I suspect she confided in you, and that with your usual generosity you gave her impeccable guidance. I admit my own cowardice on this point, and I am prepared to suffer the consequences. For four years, I thought only of myself and not much of her.

I believe Suzanne is headed toward her deepest desires and that her desires are her most profound duties.

I am leaving the city alone to look for work. I still have to pay for my children's upkeep.

I leave with my heart full, with my wife's and children's smiles in it. And I hope that my little family will be happily reunited soon.

Goodbye. Thank you for being there. I take with me the memory of a very good friend.

Letter from Marcel Barbeau to Borduas, 1952

1952—1956

You have returned to Montreal and you are drawing. You are giving charcoal classes to amateurs, in a gloomy little room that is still a breath of fresh air.

You don't know anything about charcoal, but you invent yourself as a master of the instrument.

Everyone watches you, eager for your gestures, which guide them more than your words, which you are parsimonious with.

Marcelle has given you the key to her place, where you sleep on the sofa, amidst three cats with bad breath.

In the evening she talks to you about nothing in particular, punctuating it all with laughter. She makes tomato sauce; she drinks shoplifted wine.

The wine and her levity quench your thirst.

You write while she paints, passing a plate of spaghetti back and forth between you.

You don't settle into the moment. You clutch at it and you consume it.

You know Marcel is doing odd jobs. That he spends hours on the road between Montreal and Val d'Or, passing through Rouyn, to string together hours of cabinetmaking and manual work. He sends the money to the daycare.

And yet you receive a phone call. The children can't stay there. They don't want custody of them anymore. You have to go get them. You can't. You're not ready. Marcelle helps you look for someone to go pick them up, while you find money and the space. But it's mainly courage that you're lacking.

You call Pauline, Marcel's older sister. She lives with Janine, the youngest of the Barbeau family. They are twenty-four and twenty-seven. They inspire confidence.

Pauline agrees to go get Mousse. But she doesn't have room for François. You insist: he doesn't take up much space. He's small. Just raising the subject of your son, just considering his fate, lets a splinter of maternal feeling break though. That, just that, burns you alive.

You hang up. You hang on. You choose yourself.

One is tall, thin, and blond; the other is shorter, solid, and a redhead. They walk in step.

Their words overlap. Together they create long sentences of lace.

They go into the daycare and introduce themselves: they are the Barbeau sisters. They have come to get Mousse. Mousse, who cries all the time. Mousse, who shuts herself away in closets with her little brother. Mousse, who is afraid of the boogeyman.

They find her at a table, concentrating on a drawing of an umbrella, around which she is sketching a downpour.

Her suitcase is ready, set at her side. Pauline is gentle. She takes the child by the hand. Janine is gentle too, and takes her by the other hand.

Mousse would like to grab her brother, but she has no hands free. François so small and already so alone. Stuffed in his pocket is the drawing of a blue umbrella, cleaving the pouring rain.

You are sitting with your little sister Claire, the nun. When you're with her you feel the echoes of your childhood nights. The damp nights when you opened the window to straddle its frame. Claire was your leverage, offering her frail shoulders as a ladder.

You would describe to her how the river was running, the neighbours' comings and goings, and when an English person went by, you would spit on them. So Claire would blush on your behalf, while you would burst out laughing.

Today it feels like you can see a bit of your shame on her face again. You offload your shame on her, and she carries it like a coat of arms.

You cannot stand her sad, sad eyes.

You repeat curtly that it's temporary.

You're sick of justifying yourself. You don't owe her anything. Not just yet.

You endure. You need her. You need to find someone for François. A home, temporary parents.

Claire doesn't speak. She seems to doubt you will survive.

You desert again. You will bleed to death from cutting ties like this.

You meet her eyes. She left too. To each her own means of flight.

Claire tells you she knows someone. He comes to the hospital regularly, collecting the dead. He is an undertaker. He and his wife want to adopt a child.

Your body moves from the depths to the surface. You find a wisp of voice to tell her it's perfect.

'Call them.'

A few days later, one-and-a-half-year-old François leaves the daycare in a long black car.

You exhibit your poetry. Shocking.

It stands comfortably alongside the Automatist works presented.

Journalists remark on Suzanne Barbeau's bold words that day. That is your name. Divorce is illegal in Quebec. Only men can apply for it with evidence of adultery.

Borduas approaches you from the back of the room. Something strong and intangible binds you. Broken threads. A sad connection that has gotten under your skin.

He tells you he is leaving for the United States. The evening goes on. All you want is an alcove so you can lose yourself one last time in this man's fragile body. To come together for a moment in the terrifying freedom of those who remain alone.

Mousse is four years old today.

You meet Pauline at the foot of the mountain. She is holding Mousse's hand. They still don't look alike, and that reassures you.

Mousse approaches you confidently. She is planted on the ground. She has a hard time disguising her joy at seeing you. She is bursting with it. You clear the path through it.

She says hello and calls you Mommy.

The two of you set off along Chemin Olmstead. Her small hand rests in yours as if it had never left it.

The green leaves have replaced the bursting buds, which yellow and collect on the ground like a carpet rolled out for the occasion.

You take shortcuts. You are proud to show them to her.

You have jujubes in your pocket. You sit down to share them.

Her cheeks are pink, and she looks like spring.

You tell her that she will come back to live with you. At the same time, you tell yourself the same thing.

Night is falling when you take Mousse back to her aunts. You want her to live with you. You want to watch her fall asleep. To read beside her as she dozes, her breathing slow. You want to breathe her breath in the morning. You still want to be her mother.

You knock at the door, but before they open it, Mousse takes a key out of her pocket and invites you into her house.

Yves Montand is singing full blast in the kitchen.

You walk along the orange carpet in a small hallway filled with the strong smell of warm sugar.

You walk by the tiny pink bedroom where a single large mattress accommodates three bodies. Your daughter must sleep well, nestled between two young women in their pyjamas, the smell of cottage pudding tangled in their hair.

In the kitchen, one of the sisters is at the stove. The other is at the table doing a crossword puzzle.

You are in a proper home. They invite you to stay. But feeling suddenly fragile, you offer your regrets. You have to go.

Mousse follows you to the door. You turn back and say goodbye to her like an adult.

'Goodbye.'

You close the door behind you. You won't be back.

That evening, you call Marcel. You want the children put up for adoption. To make that happen, he has to relinquish his parental rights.

He goes to the courthouse the next day and legally renounces his paternity.

Then he leaves for New York, destroyed.

Marcelle has a lover. He is tall, blue eyed and from distant lands. He likes good restaurants and the physical sciences.

He is working on a translation of *Refus Global*.

He is American, born in Chicago. But he has a distinct English accent, having grown up in the U.K.

He is ethereal. His feet touch the ground, but the rest seems to be part of the ambient air, blowing in the wind. Up where everything is possible and nothing seems serious.

You latch on to him.

You run off together.

In the classified ads of *La Presse*, you find a job ad, and you apply.

Postal worker. On the Gaspé Peninsula.

A few weeks later, you receive a job offer.

You and Peter fill a bag with a few books and clothes, and take the train to the Gaspé.

To wide-open spaces. Away from the noise. Away from your children, whose memory causes you pain.

You don't talk about it. Just hearing their names makes your stomach churn.

The train speeds along. You breathe a bit easier with the movement. You haven't changed; you are still like the horizon streaming by. You take Peter's hand. It is foreign to you. And that feels good. You feel like you could settle into it, precisely because it is unfamiliar. It speaks to you of the present. Just the present, no history, no past or future, somewhere you can stop thinking.

Peter never asks you anything about your past.

He has eyes you don't lose yourself in. Eyes that are pure surface, smooth, worry-free. That you can skim without diving in.

He smells of wet wool, of drying rain.

He has no roots, moving from encounter to encounter, a stray man.

He is curious about you. Likes watching you move and sleep. Likes the surfaces of your body. Is moved by its peculiarities. Enjoys exploring them with his soft fingers, his hot tongue.

He likes making you feel good. He becomes your hideaway. You are going into exile.

You get off the train in the Gaspé as husband and wife, strangers in a place where everyone knows each other.

A fisherman is waiting for you.

His name is Barnabas. He is the only Hungarian man in the Gaspé. He has a house to rent, right behind his.

You meet his wife Marta, the only Hungarian woman in the Gaspé. She is coming out of the smoker, where an astonishing amount of cod is drying, sliced in filets.

They don't speak English or French. But he knows how to fish and she knows how to smoke. They made this country their own.

The smell of salted fish permeates the walls of your wooden refuge, perched on the cliff.

You see the expanse of ocean in front of you, arrogant. It is so powerful, so proud. You close the curtains. You give yourself time to settle in.

The next morning, you put on your postal worker's uniform. You carry the weight of mundane correspondence on your shoulders. You enjoy learning the route, divining the contents of envelopes, becoming part of the place. Your steps take you to places where people need you. Some wait for you in the window, others in front of their house.

You feel like a conduit, and it heals you for a while.

In the evening, you go home to Peter in your house from another time. Flowered wallpaper and pastel watercolours cover the narrow walls. Peter's books are strewn everywhere, in reassuring disorder.

You eat cod. Every day. There are no vegetables or eggs here.

One day at the general store you order meat. They take out a huge red block from the freezer, which they cut with a chainsaw.

Peter cooks the meat with potatoes. It reminds him of England.

Barnabas invites you out on his boat. The open sea grabs you by the collar. You like the feeling. The wind feeds on you. Takes away your burdens for a moment. Erased.

You bring home pounds of cod, which you hang from the beams of the smokehouse with Marta. Her gestures are both coarse and feminine. She speaks to you in Hungarian, even though you can't understand her. She is carnal and energetic; her booming laugh descends on you, and sometimes you laugh too.

She is dressed in layers of faded, floral fabric, which jubilantly covers her extra few pounds.

You are dressed in black, head to toe. You've cut your hair short.

You have shrunk in this vast space.

And yet, people's eyes follow you here. Nibble at you. You have never been so visible.

Men want you, and they let you know it.

You personally hand the mail to the ones who do.

Official letters from Yale University take you to the edge of the cliff, to a patched-up little trailer.

You meet Jean, a small, energetic man with sunken cheeks and a compact body.

An agoraphobic doctoral student in theology, he is in exile and keeps the Yale Divinity School library going from here, with a view of the sea.

His trailer is as small as he is; you can't stand up in it. So you spend a few afternoons lying down with him. Salt seeps from his pores, and his hard body takes you firmly.

You leave him at sundown, the smell of sex and low tide so thick you can taste it.

Winter comes. Suddenly, with no prelude.

A storm thrashes against the walls of your house, which shakes. It will hold. It has seen others.

You huddle up against Peter. Your man-boat with whom you run aground. Who knows everything, but who asks nothing. Who harvests you anew every morning. Who rediscovers you each time.

Peter, whose smile is hung from the corner of his eyes and can't be dislodged. And who tells you about the elegance of the universe, the mysteries of anti-matter and the ultraviolet catastrophe as he sips his tea.

Peter lets you gently lose yourself in him. He knows that it is the only place you let go.

Through the winter, your bag filled with letters, you walk your route, your head into the wind, once, then again. You walk looking down at your feet, starting to miss the ocean you have grown accustomed to. It is hidden behind the blizzard, and the whole landscape disappears along with it.

You want soup and the movies.

So you hand in your resignation, and Peter packs his books in his bag.

You leave, something you know how to do so well.

The train takes you back to Montreal.

It's been only a year, but you feel like it has been more. Going back to the city upsets you. You don't like things to be permanent; it gives you vertigo. You are afraid of putting down roots again. You tell Peter you're leaving again. He says he will follow you.

You sail for Brussels, the only city in Europe that Peter has never been to.

The crossing is long and cold. You stay huddled against him. It's your first big trip.

You rent an empty room on the top floor of a building that's seen better days. You put a mattress in it. It becomes your home.

Someone is selling bags of coal in the basement. You feed a little stove that warms you and that you cook on.

You boil eggs, which you eat naked under the sheets, bathed in the acrid smell of burning coal.

You wander through the damp winter, polish the neighbourhood bars with your elbows, spend nights listening to music while smoking rolled cigarettes. You love Peter, his haughty manner, his air of great wealth despite being penniless, his levity, his keen, complex ideas. But you don't need him. And you constantly remind yourself of it.

One afternoon, you decide you want a nice dinner. You will sit in a window, cross your legs under the table. You will wear stockings and heels. Just for the occasion.

You will study the menu for a long time. Imagine the colour of the food. The texture. The smell. How it will feel on your tongue.

You may even go into the kitchen to watch how each plate is prepared before choosing the one you want.

You decide that tonight you will be a queen.

You go home and invite Peter out to eat. You can't afford such an extravagance, but Peter doesn't ask questions and that fuels your desire for him.

You choose the nicest restaurant on Place de Brouckère. A warm little alcove, a rift in the damp winter.

The young waiter gives you a seat in the window. You cross your legs under the table. You are putting the finishing touches on a graceful choreography, your gestures worthy of the moment.

You read the menu like a first novel. Delighting in pronouncing each syllable. Enjoying the words they form and the invitation they extend.

Peter wants to laugh: the romantic menu, the warmth of the place, the white tablecloth, the refinement of the waiters, you sitting up straight and intently happy.

You order pan-fried foie gras briochette, followed by guinea-fowl suprême with a porcini mushroom sauce.

You are moved by the splendour of the dishes placed before you. You breathe them in first, devouring the exquisite, astonishing odours.

You pose, then stick your fork in, consider the texture, the layers that give under the pressure, then you put what you've gathered in your mouth, alert to the flavours on your tongue, against your palate.

After months of cod and black tea, you feel like you are on an incredible journey. Peter savours the dishes with you and enjoys watching you enjoy them.

The waiter hovers over you occasionally.

'How is everything?'

You just smile at him. It is heavenly.

You enjoy the meal together, which you stretch to include dessert.

You finish your fresh fruit sabayon, slowly put on your scarf, then your black coat, and with Peter on your heels, you tell the waiter that you are going out for cigarettes. He smiles at you. He has a cousin in Canada.

It's cold outside.

You walk away slowly, gradually speeding up.

You run through the streets of Brussels, your stomach full and your mouth still excited at having tasted so much.

Winded in the stairwell of your shabby building, you kiss Peter, who is taller than you, whom you love but don't need.

You make love in your dark room, and you tell him that tomorrow you will find a job.

The next day, you knock on doors. You offer your services as a secretary. You know how to handle ink, and you have to pay the rent.

But you don't find a job.

Peter asks for an advance from his parents, who send him a bit of money and two train tickets to London. They miss him. Come while you figure out what to do next, they say.

You leave your room in Belgium and head for England.

Liz and Arthur live in a small apartment on the sixth floor of a tower on the outskirts of London.

They are old and laugh a lot, both together and apart.

Liz likes fish. She collects aquariums, which are scattered around the house.

Arthur likes to sing. He is in the neighbourhood choir, something he takes seriously, and spends five or six hours a day rehearsing his parts.

They are happy to be reunited with their son and delighted to meet you.

You have tea with Liz and help her fry the meat she serves at every meal.

You sleep in Peter's boyhood room. There is still quite a collection of comic books in it. He dives into them, first with a quick glance, then with undisguised pleasure.

You soon feel the need to extract yourself from this family that wants to become yours. You buy a bus pass and explore London.

You get lost a few times before finding your home away from home: the National Gallery.

The museum is huge and brightly lit. You breathe easier here than in the rest of the city.

You spend entire days in it.

The lanky man who guards the entrance knows you now. He greets you by name: 'Hello, Suze.' You don't put anything in the cloakroom because now you are a fugitive. You leave no trace.

On your first few visits, you gave each piece equal attention, lingering over the name and the artist's ideas, but now you forge a free, anarchic path. You walk through the museum to the end, where you spend hours in front of *The Tempest*. 1862. An overcast sky. Filled with threatening clouds, an impending storm contained within. You find the promise of a cyclone restful. The fact that someone, the artist Peder Balke in this case, was willing to wait for it, patiently stationed below it, makes you love people. You would have happily waited for that storm by his side. You could have plastered your back against the artist's, and neck to neck, you would have taken on the sky.

Sometimes you bring a book with you, flipping through it distractedly while sitting on a bench, and sometimes you fall asleep. Some days, nothing. You just sit there, in the vast, echoing space, where you feel almost at home.

You bring fruit and bread with you. You station yourself under *Cognoscenti in a Room Hung with Pictures* to eat slowly. Young people, paintbrushes in hand, are spread out in an atelier. Their frozen bodies in the midst of the painting. The lively space reminds you of Borduas's living room. You think of Marcel. But not for too long.

You think about what you would have painted if you really wanted to. But not for too long.

One afternoon, Peter joins you. It's noon. He knows he will find you under the Flemish painting, in front of the vibrant atelier that reminds you of your other life. He has nougat.

He tells you that you should paint. You make a face. He laughs.

That evening, he brings you a piece of blank canvas. A real one. Without any traces of motor oil.

While his father sings and his mother fries supper, you shut yourself in the boyhood bedroom of this man who is taking care of you, and you paint for the first time in a long time.

You paint for hours, and they leave you to it.

You open the door at around midnight to go to the bathroom. Peter has fallen asleep on the coach. You walk by him without looking at him. Then you stop and lie down on top of him. You run your paint-stained hand over his freshly shaven cheek. You want to make love to him because you don't know how to say thank you.

You want to make love to him here, in the middle of his family's living room, amid the aquariums and begonias.

You take out his cock and put it in your mouth.

In Peter's childhood bedroom there is a painting that later you will name *Le pont Mirabeau* and that will be exhibited at the Musée d'art contemporain de Montréal.

One morning in 1956, you run to take refuge at the museum.

Peter finds you there that night, under Cranach's *Charity*. The one you practically run by. The one you studiously avoid.

Now, under the image of this young, prosperous woman, a child at her breast, two others thriving at her feet, you tremble.

You don't bother lifting your eyes to Peter when he leans over you. You tell him in a surprisingly clear voice that he has to find money.

You are thirty years old. You are pregnant.

Abortion is still illegal in 1956. There are a number of ways around that.

Alcohol-soaked parsley, which is inserted into the vagina, until the fetus is expelled.

Violently jumping up and down for twenty-four hours, until the fetus is expelled.

A long knitting needle inserted in the vagina and turned to the left, then the right, to expel the fetus.

They are all common methods. You can do them alone and risk death or pay someone to do them for you and risk death slightly less.

Peter asks his parents for money for a university class, and you pay a backstreet abortionist to empty your belly.

You go to her house. The wind gusts through it. Or else it's howling inside your body. Behind your messy hair, your face is smooth. Expressionless. This ability of yours to disassociate, to detach from your body. Your stomach is a war zone, but your eyes are blank. The lights are out.

She points to the couch, and you lie down. It is rough against your skin. A texture that takes you back to Peter's living room. Where you swallowed him. You think about that. Fast. You take refuge around Peter's long, hard cock.

She sticks the needle in your body.

You think about the trembling that starts at the top of his thighs, which you brush with your fingertips.

She rotates the needle. She is fishing.

You think about the flash of red in his hair. The briny taste that gradually coats his penis.

She is speaking to you, but you don't hear her.

It burns.

You think about the grateful animal breath. You run your tongue over his cock. You leave no trace. Never leave a trace.

She says it's over. She brushes your cheek with the back of her hand to wipe away a tear. She washes a rag red with blood and continues wiping along your thighs. She pulls your panties back up and slips a rolled towel inside them. She goes over the possible complications, which run through your mind like a song. She puts your coat over your shoulders. She asks you whether you have anyone to help you. She asks you whether you want a cup of tea. She opens the door. She helps you navigate the stairs.

Outside, Peter is waiting for you, smoking. He takes you by the hand. You would have liked him to say something, but he doesn't.

You don't stay in bed. You don't even cry. You change your underwear, and you tell Peter you're going home.

Montreal hasn't changed. But after London, the city seems younger. Childlike, unfinished. The naïvete feels good. You feel like you're starting out too.

You find a couch at the friend of a friend's, and you come ashore there for a few days.

It's spring and the city is waking up. But you just want to sleep.

One morning, the wilted buds on the staircase make you think of your daughter. She is eight or nine now.

There is a phone booth at the corner of the street. You take refuge in there. You dial the number almost without realizing it. Janine or Pauline answers.

'Hello?'

'Hi. It's Suzanne. Suzanne Meloche.'

'Suzanne! How are you?'

'Is Mousse there?'

'Yes, she's here.'

Mousse comes out of her bedroom. She is nine years old. She is tiny, her hair is jet black, her face is round, her eyes are piercing. Her front tooth is loose. She hopes that tonight the tooth fairy will be able to come and collect it. Mousse believes in the tooth fairy, even though she is nine years old. She also believes in Santa Claus and the Easter Bunny. By choice. Mousse likes magic. She needs it.

Frozen in the middle of the kitchen, she is hanging on the lips of her Aunt Pauline. Her mother is on the phone. She has a drawing for her. No, two drawings. She knows a new song too, which she learned at school. And she got a good grade on her French composition.

'London? Lucky you. You must have loved it … '

Aunt Pauline looks at Mousse. Smiles at her. Aunt Pauline is nice. When she wears her pink flowered nightgown, she seems even nicer.

'She's right here. Do you want to talk to her?'

Mousse wants to talk to her mother. She has wanted to talk to her since she was a little girl. She left before she could really talk to her. And now she speaks well. She knows plenty of words, and she uses them well. They tell her so at school. Mousse wants to speak to her, but her steps retreat rather than advancing toward Pauline, who is holding out the receiver.

But Pauline is nice and she waits.

Mousse makes the decision. Walks as if she were walking along a wire. What word should she start with? She has missed her mother so much. She missed everything. There is so much to tell.

'Hello?'

'Hello … Mousse?'

Silence.

'How are you?'

'Okay.'

At the other end of the line, there is graffiti in the phone booth. *Eat shit* written in marker. *Motherfucker*. There should be lace. There should be a carpet and velvet curtains. You need a chair, a chair to sit down on.

'Mousse, it's me. It's Suzanne.'

Your daughter's voice. You want to smell her breath. As a reflex, you press your nose up to the phone. Your mouth too.

Mousse asks you whether you had a nice trip. She is articulate. Her words sound pretty spoken in her voice. You tell her that yes, you had a nice trip. She asks whether you are coming to see her. You hold the phone with both hands. You press it to your face, want to melt inside of it. You tell her yes. In her silence, you hear that she is happy and scared. Like you. Aunt Pauline takes the phone back.

And you tell Pauline that you want Mousse back. You want her with you. You want to learn the song of her voice by heart. You want to see her hair grow too long and trim her bangs, trying hard to get them straight. You want to know the depth of her dimples and the curve of her forehead. You want to touch the texture of her little girl tears when you comfort her. You want. Right now.

In the small apartment that smells of cottage pudding, Aunt Pauline turns gently toward Mousse. She looks her right in the eye.

She asks her, since she is a big girl, whether she wants to go back to live with her mother.

Mousse is nine years old. She is not a big girl. Aunt Janine arrives in the doorway. She is wearing blue pyjamas. Aunt Pauline stares at Mousse. Aunt Pauline is nice. Aunt Janine too. In the morning they smell like cottage pudding with cinnamon. Mousse puts her hand in her mouth and wiggles her tooth. Back and forth back and forth back and forth.

In the phone booth you are waiting you are cold all of a sudden it's winter *Motherfucker* screams in your face.

The tooth gives way in Mousse's hand. Mousse holds the tooth in her hand.

Aunt Pauline repeats the question.

Mousse says no. And she runs to her bedroom to put the tooth that has just fallen out under her pillow.

You hang up. You leave the phone booth. Your shoelace is not untied but you tie it anyway. You try to figure out where to go. You are falling and you don't know when it will stop.

You take the train to get your balance.

You take the train to New York, a city you don't know.

1956—1965

Her voice slides through you like sand slips through an hourglass. It creeps in, then winds up inhabiting you. You open your eyes. You wake up.

You are still on the park bench. Night has fallen.

There are young Black girls in front of you. You notice her among the others. She reigns. Her endless legs make her sway gently. Her body is a swollen, proud sail, her neck arched like a tree trunk, her eyes so black that they get lost in the night. She is looking at you.

You surface. You sit up.

You fell asleep in Central Park. The city's laboured breath around you reassures you.

The young woman approaches you, shouting at you in English. 'Who are you?'

Yet her bitter presence reveals a tear. A queen unhinged, crowned with scrap iron, who is offering you a swig of beer. Asking you what you are doing there.

Your throat is dry. The beer feels good.

You answer. You arrived from Montreal. You took the train, got off, and this is where you find yourself. You don't know what's next.

She smiles. She likes your story. She introduces herself: Selena.

The other girls have drawn closer. A small sparkling herd around her, the alpha female. She tells you to follow her. She knows a place you can sleep.

You stand, draw up to her side, step into her delicate aura. You want to follow her. You join her crew, and you all follow her.

You head into Harlem.

Two thirty-seven 122nd Street. Harlem is Black. Exclusively. You know it. You feel it as you head in. And once again you are an intruder. A role you know well. The feeling of not belonging. You've had it since childhood. You know it so well it reassures you. You feel like you are in familiar territory: different.

Selena is delighted with the situation but takes it seriously. She has brought a young white woman into her neighbourhood. She looks out for you.

She opens door 237, which leads to a staircase, which the peeling grey walls make look as though they're narrowing as they climb.

Several floors rise up in the darkness. Selena knocks on the first door in front of her. An old Black man, with a gaunt face and half-closed eyes, opens the door.

Selena hugs him affectionately. She reaches toward a series of hooks and grabs a key.

She takes you upstairs.

The stairs creak under your feet. Behind closed doors, a burst of wailing from a television or a heated discussion. Hoarse, burnt voices combine in a language that brings you back to the wet soil, your feet sinking into it, to your tumultuous river.

Selena opens the door to number 18.

A group of junkies used to exist there. They are dead or disappeared. You can stay there.

A cursory cleaning was done, but the odour of excess and despair still hangs in the air.

There is a mattress in the middle of the room.

In a corner, there is a small aquarium where an iguana is resting.

Selena holds her hand out, asking, victoriously, for a share of the rent. Clearly, she's given you white woman's rates. That will pay for her next binge.

Then she hesitates a little, scanning your face. And as if she found motivation in your features, she warns you.

'It's dangerous for a white woman here.'

You tell her that's fine with you. You're not afraid.

That's not quite the case. It's more that you accept being put in danger. You almost want it. Deserve it.

Selena, royal and ungrounded, stares at you. She understands. An uncomfortable connection passes between you.

She smiles at you. Wishes you good luck.

The door closes. Shutting you in.

You pull on the sheet hung as a curtain, revealing the street. A couple is walking down it with their arms around each other, a hand slipped in the other's pocket, as one.

A few kids are hanging around a garbage can in which a fire is crackling. Its black smoke splits the sky.

You have deserted. You pulled on your roots. There's blood. But you don't bandage the wound. You will swim in your blood until you bleed out.

Selena's laugh, as she crosses the street, rises to reach you. She is leaving, followed by her armada of young, proud women. She glances at your window. You bow your head almost imperceptibly. Your skin's lunar glow announces your presence to the whole street. Selena waves to you.

You sleep on your stomach, arms open, legs too, as if you had just landed after a long fall, having been caught by a yellowed mattress in the middle of the night.

The world is already coming alive outside when you open your eyes.

The iguana stares at you.

It is inviting you to stay. But you are afraid of standing still. It's when you're moving that you feel your chains. They comfort you as you run away.

You don't unpack, ready to leave at any moment.

In the months that follow, you will travel without incident from 122nd Street in Harlem to the studio of Jean-Paul Riopelle, who has made it in the big city. He has his shows, his friends, his habits. He invites you into his life. But it doesn't appeal to you. You want to paint in silence, and he gives you the opportunity.

In his large Manhattan studio, on the concrete floor, he opens the doors to whoever wants to come in. Young students and seasoned painters can be found there, crouching and abandoned, but you aren't interested in them.

You avoid the looks and flee the conversations. You spend hours wearing out your knees on the rough floor, your neck at a right angle, your body open over a canvas that will become your territory.

You empty and free yourself onto it; you vomit yourself whole and in colour until the early morning hours, when you often leave last, returning to your Black neighbourhood, cheating death every time.

Because Harlem has not yet eaten you alive. Every day you endure reactions to the haughty whiteness that you trail behind you on the sidewalk. People heckle and harass you, steal from you and spit in your face. *White whore is in town.*

You just don't care. Something in you feeds on the rejection.

But one night when someone is following you too closely, you take refuge in a phone booth.

And you dial Marcel's number. A woman answers. With her high voice, she asks who is calling.

'It's Suzanne.'

Silence. You imagine her floating over to Marcel. You, who had lead feet. She must be soft with him.

Marcel answers. He seems far away. But his furtive voice is the voice of too-raw emotions.

You just want to tell him you still exist. You are afraid to ask whether he has seen the children.

Mousse came to spend a day in the studio. She ate oysters with him.

'On a tablecloth?'

That's the question you ask. You want a clear image. Of a picnic between father and daughter. Of a single meal, an ephemeral connection to your fractured lives.

'What about François?'

Marcel doesn't know where your baby is. He was taken to somewhere in Abitibi. Where a family of undertakers witnessed his first steps.

You hang up the phone and trail your pain back to your lair, where Selena is waiting for you.

She is lying on your mattress, half naked. She is polishing off a bottle of rum. Sweat beads on her emaciated torso.

So you sink into her. She founders in you.

Pained and famished, you swallow each other. You taste her sweet skin, suck her large, rippled sex. She explores you savagely, scarifies your abandoned body.

And between two breaths, you let your pain show. Mid-caress you wail your emptiness.

Selena wraps herself around you and licks you. And talks about herself.

Her children. Her premature twins. Two little Black bodies latched on her breast, their breath growing weaker as one … Two little bodies too Black to be saved. The doctors who watch them slowly die because the incubator is *Whites only*, kept in the White wing of the hospital, where they don't let people die.

The weight of her two children leaving a permanent imprint, *there*. She presses her palms into her stomach.

That's it. That's where you form one. Eviscerated.

You sleep in each other's arms.

At Jean-Paul's studio, Jackson Pollock is lord and master. Awestruck disciples mill around without ever approaching him. He bites.

You don't care.

You hurl your self-destruction on the new canvas. You follow the anarchic metronome of your guts that can only come undone here.

One evening, you run out of black paint. But the white of the canvas seems to be vanishing, and you feel the distinct need to tie it down with thick black.

It's four in the morning. The only people left are you and Jackson. He is at the opposite end of the studio, dozing in a haze of alcohol, huddled against a still damp painting.

You creep up to him, linger for a moment over his rough, resting face. He isn't moving, and yet everything about him still seems to be fighting. His broad nose and his bare forehead give him the sad look of a boxer on the mat. You fall for a moment into the small cleft in his chin. You don't know why, but he makes you want to cry. You make yourself small and snuggle up against him, lost in the remnants of childhood in his angry face.

You grab the dregs of the black paint lying at the foot of the sleeping giant. And you stride back across the room.

You finish your painting with Jackson's paint.

It is seven in the morning when you leave the studio, leaving the damp canvas behind you. You won't be back.

The painting, entitled *Métronome*, will be exhibited at the Montreal spring salon. It was picked up in the morning by Jackson, who thought it was tragic, and fabulous.

On February 22, 1960, Borduas dies in Paris. You see his face in black and white, reduced to a tiny picture in the Births and Deaths section of a New York paper. You aren't sad. But a powerful wave of anger washes over you. You are mad at him. Abstractly, but deeply.

You are mad at him for having let you go. You are mad at him for not having chosen you, for not having kept you. You are mad at him for having let you believe that you were a special person, in special times.

There is something sour in the air. The smell of rising waters. The smell of contained anger. Harlem is finally erupting. Harlem is spilling out of its emaciated neighbourhood.

First you notice that there are more Black people in the street. They are walking with purpose, headed somewhere. You don't remember seeing such a clear sense of direction here before. There is no trace of aimless wandering. It's a clear path that stretches to the horizon.

You advance, alone, and you feel more scattered than them, whose ranks are swelling before your eyes. Then they disperse and come back together.

And, suddenly, something snaps. Nothing you can hear. Nothing you can see. An inaudible call, and yet so clear. The peaceful crowd reacts to it. Explodes.

Windows smashing. One, then ten, then hundreds.

Harlem has jumped its banks, a river of naphtha. The city goes up in flames.

New York is burning, ripped apart.

Cars that dare drive into the magma of rage are set on fire. Stores are emptied, pillaged. Children emerge from them, their arms filled with whatever they can find. Salami, toilet paper, socks.

Old women stumble, tangled up in their bags filled with frozen food. Victory cries mingle with political demands.

You hug the walls, you cross the storm, intimidated by the chaos that inspires you and draws you in.

They have taken over space. From the ground up, buildings are consumed; Black faces emerge from them, victorious. They conquer the city in turn.

You envy the people walking by, a child on their shoulders, their cries carrying farther thanks to the piece of eternity they have on their backs.

Mousse's weight suddenly lands on you. Would you be able to carry her on your shoulders, her two little knees framing your jaw, her pretty hands running a path through your hair?

You stumble. At your feet is a panting cat. Around the cat is a constellation of pink kittens, still wet. They have just been born. Passersby jostle you. If the cats stay there, they will die.

You take off your jacket and wrap them in it.

Their claws prick your arms. You advance through the storm, your living cargo pressed against your gut.

A man is being beaten; spread-eagled on the ground, under the weight of two policeman, he is struggling, enraged.

An eager child watches him, emptying a bag of stolen chips into his mouth.

You feel the warm weight of the cats against you.

You are looking for a path. You are looking for an exit. The cat and her kittens have become the focus of your life. What still matters.

An alley. You slip into it. You find a den to hide your survivors in.

You kneel down, gently spread out your jacket, which the mother escapes from, scared. You watch her go. She is headed toward the heaving street, her bottom bloody, her breasts full.

You put the frightened kittens on your bloody jacket; their hoarse meows make you anxious. With a trembling voice, you try to reassure them. Then a hard blow knocks you to the ground.

A heavy weight on your jaw, which cracks.

'White whore, get out of here.'

You open your eyes, looking for the source, glance at the Black faces with fine, crazed features. Young women. A pastiche of Amazons in a fury, growling, bent over you, astonished wolves. You try to protect the kittens, curl up in a ball.

'This is our war, nigger lover.'

The final salvo. Your bones crack and sink into the hot asphalt.

Total darkness. Which you tumble into.

Your door and window are shut. You don't go out anymore. You don't sleep anymore. The remains of a riot linger outside, growing fainter every day, put down with increasing violence by the police.

Night finally lets sleep overtake you, and you surrender to it for a few hours.

When you wake up, you see Selena in your kitchen, a bowl of cereal in hand. She holds it out to you, and you wolf it down. You haven't eaten in days.

She doesn't say anything, but she examines the bruises on your face, which are slowly fading.

'You look great.'

She asks you to go out.

Her light spreads over you and almost burns your skin. She casts a spell on you.

In a small room, White people and Black people, mixing together and packed in. They are in their twenties and are hanging on the words of an older man, who stops speaking when you arrive. You are late. Faces turn toward you.

You already regret being there. You have a bitter sense of déjà vu. A master with his young disciples, thirsty for possibility.

A shared purpose emerges under the harsh neon lights.

You recognize this silent agitation, and you don't want anything to do with it anymore. Selena feels it and tightens her warm hold on you.

The man greets you. He knows Selena by name and bids you a warm welcome.

Your head is spinning. You have the sordid impression of recognizing the gentle face of your attackers, scattered through the audience.

You hang on to Selena, who finds you a seat, where you land. She sits in front of you.

At the front, the man is continuing his speech. After landing, you don't listen to him right away. You check out the room. You try to recognize parts of the vicious bodies who beat you senseless. But your eye comes to rest on Selena's slender neck. And all of these Black bodies become hers.

At the front, Farmer – that's his name – methodically goes through the itinerary for the upcoming trip.

You have never seen such a mix of colours. White people and Black people have come together, in a soup of protestors. The simple fact of raising questions together, under the same roof, is a minor revolution.

While paper and pencils are passed around the assembly, the Freedom Ride is summed up for you.

It takes you back to your childhood, at the back of the class, watching the attentive, still necks, that you find moving in their fragility.

And the hardened neck of Selena. Who grabs you and pulverizes you. Her clay neck, so straight. The refined neck of an injured woman.

At the front, he continues: two integrated buses. Filled with Blacks and Whites. Blacks and Whites together. Touching each other. Breathing each other in. Cutting across the States to the Deep South, armed with the explosive hubris of togetherness.

Someone holds out a blank sheet of paper to you.

'No real risk. But better to do it,' Selena whispers in your ear. 'Just in case.'

Just in case. A will.

You are dumbstruck for a moment.

You have nothing to leave anyone. And no one to say goodbye to. Looking at the blank sheet, you take stock of your solitude. You come to terms with it and carry it like a flag. You have nothing, no one. You are free. You pass the empty sheet on.

Prospective stops: Washington, Richmond, Greensboro, Columbia, Atlanta. Then ... Anniston and Birmingham, Alabama. Alabama: the Johannesburg of the States. Where the Ku Klux Klan reigns. No protest movement has ever gone that far. The goal is clear and decided: to inflame the South. To provoke a crisis.

You hurt everywhere. In your gutted, crazed stomach, in all the white fragments of your unloved skin, in the blood that pounds in your temples and in the blue marks that cover your face, your thighs, your back, and that scream, *You don't belong*.

But in front of you, the black neck of a giant woman stretches before you, a hyena woman with her guts torn out, the sharp-edged neck that hisses its vengeance. The neck like an arrow that turns toward you, revealing to you the moving softness of her childlike features.

'Come.'

You cling to her pride.

You are ready to plunge in wherever she asks.

'Okay.'

You will travel the miles together. You will be the white half of your *fuck you*.

The bus leaves tomorrow. It will be a two-week trip.

Your reflection is superimposed on the passing road. In that in-between place where you breathe easiest. The desire to be part of something is gently reborn inside you.

You are sitting near the window. America is passing before your eyes. In the bus, they are singing a traditional gospel song.

> I'll ask my brother, come go with me.
>> I'm on my way, great God, I'm on my way.
> If he won't come, I'll go alone.
>> I'm on my way, great God, I'm on my way.
> I'll ask my sister, come go with me.
>> I'm on my way, great God, I'm on my way.
> If she won't come, I'll go anyhow.
>> I'm on my way, great God, I'm on my way.
> I'm on my way to the freedom land.
>> I'm on my way, great God, I'm on my way.

A roadside diner. You go in, alternating Black White Black White. Hanging over the back section, there is a sign yellowed by grease splatters that reads *Colored Only*.

You all sit at the counter. Under the *Whites Only* sign. The young waitress freezes, plates in hand. She watches you take your seats, horrified. She glances at the cooks, who have stopped moving.

The other diners are also in suspense.

'Hello, Miss. I'll have a burger and fries, please. And a lemonade.'

The waitress snaps out of it, babbles a few words, then nervously jots down the order. Her eyes land on you. You hold back a smile.

'Same thing. Same as my friend,' you add, a bit theatrically.

The waitress jots that down and then takes the other orders, clutching her pencil, the weight of the world on her shoulders.

Behind her, one of the cooks grumbles that he doesn't cook for 'niggers.'

But gradually all the plates wind up on the counter. You relish your first victory in silence.

A jar of pickled beets sits in front of you. You pull it over and plunge your hand in.

No one here knows about your past life.

You put a sweet beet in your mouth. Force yourself to swallow it without batting an eye.

Selena slides a hand along your thigh, squeezes it lovingly, smiles at you.

Here, you are new.

You feel almost happy.

You take your seat on the bus. Your seat. If you weren't there, it would be empty. You struggle with the idea. You are becoming part of a group.

Trees are moving beneath your white reflection in the window. You're hot. Your damp thighs stick to the seat. A terrible feeling of déjà vu. A trip to nowhere in the heat of a day like any other. Mousse too close to you. Her pale little thigh brushing up against yours. You pulling back a few centimetres, foreshadowing the imminent rupture; you retreat from her little body, which is too soft, too much yours.

Your stomach hurts.

You don't want to think. Soon you fall asleep on Selena's shoulder.

They strike up a new gospel song, which lulls you until the next stop.

It's sunny outside. The two buses are crossing through the invisible gateway to Alabama together. A faded but solidly planted official sign is all that awaits you: *Welcome to Alabama. We dare defend our rights.*

The atmosphere is light, and already there is a sense of minor victory in the air.

Then a car passes you. There are two ghosts aboard. You had only ever seen them in pictures. There they are, passing you and driving a few centimetres away from you.

Your throat gets dry. The piercing eyes of the Ku Klux Klan, under the spotless hoods, have looked at you.

The bus is forced to stop. The car is blocking it. Selena presses up against you. You look at the car, from which five hooded people emerge, with disconcerting grace.

You look around. Are you alone? A few steps from the road there is a small gas station, a minimart, a few cars. In front of you there are men. A few women and children too.

So you have not been abandoned. There is hope. You whisper to Selena that it will be okay. You have witnesses.

There is a pop, followed by a high-pitched whistle: the tires, slashed.

The beginnings of panic around you. You get up, head toward the door, signal to the driver to open it for you.

'I'll talk to them.'

Your skin gives you strength. They won't hurt you. You're white. But from the hordes at the gas station, someone shouts. A woman.

'Let's burn them niggers!'

You turn toward the source of the shout. You look each other up and down through the window. She may be forty. Two young kids hang on her skirt. She is pretty. She shouts again.

'Kill them nigger lovers!'

That's when you start to understand the small crowd. Revealed by this maternal voice. Her shout a carbon copy of the reality forming in front of you: men, women, and children. Armed. With crowbars. Hammers. Pickaxes.

The five ghosts from the KKK have joined the agitated group. An anonymous hand emerges from a white robe to light a torch.

The gas tank explodes. Screams of panic. Smoke quickly fills the space. You are choking. But they are waiting for you outside.

You close your eyes and grope your way to the front.

Selena grabs on to you like a child. You push her to the floor. Where you can still breathe. The front door opens. You spill out.

Thick air greets you. You swallow it like someone who is thirsty. Still blinded by the smoke, you can't make out what's around you.

Then, roaring in the soft light of the spring, the horde pounces on you.

'Kill them nigger lovers!'

Slim calves, a bandage on a knee. Untied shoelaces. A child bashes you on the neck with a stick.

You go down.

A silhouette is running between the scattered bodies. It doesn't move like the others. It is floating, stopping at the feet of every fallen body. It offers water from a bottle that is already almost empty. It draws closer to you, bends over, scared. Blond hair sticks to the damp face. She is six or seven years old. Terror is stamped on her face. As you swallow the few lifesaving drops, you tell yourself that she will never be free of it. That forevermore she will be disfigured by this day.

She is off, jumping nervously from body to body, finding a bit of balance while she offers a gulp.

Suddenly, a deep voice. An appeal.

'Okay. That's enough now. You've had your fun.'

From his horse, his voice carried by the megaphone, a policeman finally calls for calm.

And slowly, obediently, the crowd disperses.

A few minutes later, only your group is left.

You survey the scene. A shower of broken bodies, crumpled on the ground, in the light of the setting sun.

Selena is in the fetal position. Slowly she catches her breath. Then, with an unhurried, expansive movement, she unfolds toward the sky. She gets up, splitting the horizon. Ready to carry on.

So you get up too.

You tear yourself off the ground, although your outline remains, an affront to the well-tended lawn.

The carcass of the bus is still smoking at the side of the road. You have nowhere to go.

You advance as one, without touching one another, cutting through the hypocritical suburb that pretends not to see you, a slaughtered group of people dragging their heels, nervously looking behind them, fearing an ambush.

You need to find somewhere to sleep.

The houses grow fewer and farther between, and their absence comforts you.

A large house stands alone on the side of the road. It is different from the others somehow. It is rickety and asymmetrical, which makes it seem less hostile.

You knock on the door. Selena and Farmer go with you.

A thin man in a bathrobe opens the door a crack.

'We've been attacked.'

The man gives you a quick once-over. You feel him hesitating. He looks at the group waiting behind you. He is afraid. But he asks you to come in.

You are squeezed into the living room, a close-knit group that can't quite fill the space, even though there is plenty of it and it's comfortable.

The man seems to have disappeared. His wife, slim and elegant in silk pyjamas, puts the contents of her medicine cabinet at your disposal so you can bandage your wounds.

She hands out tomato sandwiches, then sits down beside you.

She had heard about you. About your bus. She knows what happened.

She is intelligent. You know it. You feel it.

She talks to you in a soft, maternal voice. Tells you that you shouldn't come here upsetting things. That you are making a mistake.

'The niggers, you know, we like them … We get along …'

It's a good sandwich. Predictable and reassuring. You eat it and ask for another. There are family photos on the walls around you. You count four children. Vacation smiles, graduation smiles, wedding smiles.

Happy smiles marking an ordinary life.

And suddenly, you ask if you can make a call.

The telephone is sitting on a small bedside table. You sit on the edge of the bed. On one of the large pink flowers that adorn the quilt. The woman, who is sensitive, smiles at you and closes the door behind her.

You dial. You expect to get one of the Barbeau sisters. Pauline or Janine, whom you mix up anyway. But Mousse answers. Her voice is making its way from childhood to adulthood. Why isn't she at school?

It's the first thing you say to her.

A fraction of you is still intact, a maternal part salvaged.

At the other end of the line, time like a chasm.

'Mommy?'

You don't know how to answer that question.

So Mousse throws herself into this special moment.

She speaks slowly and draws out her words to make her story last a lifetime.

No, she's not at school. She has a fever. Yesterday she went to the movies with a boy. He put his thumb in her mouth. He touched her tongue. She liked it. Then he got closer to her. He smelled good. The salted butter from warm popcorn. And he kissed her, on the mouth, for a long time. She came back home. In love and with a fever. That's why she isn't at school.

Sitting on a large flowery bed. An ordinary mother.

You hear Mousse's smile. She continues her story so as not to lose you again. She tells you that since the kiss, her hair has gone curly. She asks you whether yours gets curly too.

Someone knocks at the door. It's Farmer. He has to make a call. It's urgent.

You lie to Mousse and tell her yes. Yours gets curly too.

You hang up and you die a little.

Farmer spends hours on the phone. He is doing his best to reach the other bus. No one knows whether it kept going. Whether it made it across Alabama. Whether it is sitting somewhere in ashes.

You will get your answer the next day, when you join the rest of the troops, crammed together in the jail in Jackson, Mississippi.

The police are at the door.

You are arrested for disorderly conduct.

There are eight of you in a cell for two.

The Whites have been separated from the Blacks, locked up at opposite ends of the jail.

One by one, they come get you. Strip-search you.

In an empty, cold room, a pair of gloved hands penetrates you. You stare at the concrete wall that is holding you up. You hang on to its bumps. Its short cracks, its craters. Small dried-up lakes. Like on the moon. You settle into them while a strange hand searches inside you.

The search is over. You wipe the Vaseline left between your legs with the back of your hand. You turn to face the young woman with fine features who stares at you in disdain. She takes you back to your cell and shoves you hard into those who have become your people.

Now you understand that worse than the Blacks are those who like them. *Dirty Whites*, and you are one of them.

On the floor is a carpet of newspapers. The sheets pile up under your feet, then under your slumped, crammed bodies. News from America.

Hours pass during which you can't guess what will happen next.

Then metal dishes are handed around, a gruel of cooked vegetables congealing in them. You are so hungry.

You sleep entangled. You are assaulted by the smell of rancid breath.

Days and nights go by without you being able to wash.

You don't talk anymore to avoid smelling each other.

You all hear wailing from the other end of the jail. Or maybe you are the only one who hears it.

One night, you dream of Mousse.

She has breasts. Two little breasts poking through her Donald Duck T-shirt. You wake up with a start.

You throw up in a corner. You call for Selena, with what voice you have left. But no one comes. You end up curling up and think, in that moment, that you could finish dying.

You hardly talk anymore, or only when looking at the ground. Like when you were little and you walked with your head bent over the new shoes your father had given you. You are once again thrown into that place where there is no horizon.

A crash: a wall explodes, a pyrotechnic woman races across the damp hall. She slows down as she gets to you. She casts a crazed look your way. It electrifies you. Hilda Strike, a blazing fantasy continuing her never-ending race, quenching your thirst. You watch her as she disappears.

And you keep your head up.

Then, at the end of the hall, steps. It's unexpected. They come closer and pass by you. Ten, eleven, twelve … Whites and Blacks. They are marching, loyal and proud. They advance, making the sign of victory with their fingers barely hidden in their empty pockets.

Your vacant bodies, suspended, let them go by and disappear. A fleeting, mysterious apparition.

But a few hours later, it happens again.

Around fifteen young people, the smell of victory in their wake.

Then you understand. That the tide has turned. That now they are arriving in waves, Blacks and Whites, coming from across America, to encourage you. To split the walls of Parchman, which is gradually filling up.

And for the first time in your life, you feel like someone.

They would have done it without you. They would have won without you. But at that point in your life, you needed them. And, maybe, they needed you a little.

On August 28, 1961, three hundred new demonstrators were jailed in Parchman.

On September 22, 1961, the Kennedy administration ordered the release of detainees in the prison that was bursting at the seams, at the same time as he declared the use of segregationist signs *Colored* and *Whites Only* illegal.

From your little office in the heart of Greenwich Village, you finish drafting a pamphlet encouraging activists and politicians to join a demonstration two days later. Your fingers fly over the typewriter, graceful despite the routine.

You are a secretary for an activist association. For the first time in a long while, you have habits. Your black boots, your lipstick, your two morning coffees.

You are celebrating your fortieth birthday today. You don't tell anyone. Selena knows and calls you from the hospital room where she has just given birth to her first child. A boy, born the same day as you; she wants you to meet him.

You will go. Not so much to see him as to see her, filled with milk and armed with new power and vulnerability.

You leave the office and make a detour to the liquor store to buy a bottle of champagne.

There is a young man in front of the store. Sitting on the ground, his back resting against a public bench, his head between his knees and his hand out.

There are plenty just like him in New York. But something about him speaks to you. Maybe his stillness. It seems almost fake, rigid in the midst of staccato steps. Only the slight trembling of his hand gives away the life inside him.

You go in. You choose the finest champagne. And you pass by him again, avoiding looking at him. Convinced, this time, that he is looking at you too.

A quick stop at your apartment on the third floor of an old building in Manhattan.

You put on some music. 'My Guy,' by Mary Wells.

You dance while you're changing.

The phone rings. It's your sister, Claire. Her voice hesitates as the cheerful music reaches her ears.

'Mom is dead.'

In your mind, your mother is your age. You want to see her old. You want to see her dead. You desperately need that finality.

'I'll come.'

You head to the hospital.

Climb the steps to the maternity ward. Push on the glass doors.

But you are more of an alien amid the mothers than amid the Blacks, and you won't go in.

This is where you abandon Selena, who will live without you now. She is becoming a mother, whereas you are becoming an orphan.

You turn on your heels.

You crisscross the city, a dry crater in your chest.

You don't need anyone. But the ground already feels shakier under your feet.

You find yourself in front of him. The young, still man. Fossilized. He is sleeping stretched out on the bench. His hands, which move you, still have a tremor.

You sit down beside him. He opens his eyes and stares at you. His face is impassive, and his eyes grab on to you.

He must be twenty years old. An urge bubbles to the surface to take him and rock him. You smile at him. You take the bottle out of your bag; you open it and hold it out to him. The golden foam runs over his hands, which finally stop moving, grabbing on to the lifeline you are holding out to him.

He drinks.

You tell him it's your birthday. He drinks again. He wishes you a happy birthday and introduces himself. Gary.

He will be the third man in your life. And the last.

1965–1974

Summer 1964, Journal of Corporal Adams (Excerpts)

The night was thick. I had slugs in my shoes. They were squished between my toes. I had stopped removing them, I was so used to their soft, wet presence. I even surprised myself by talking to them. Asking them what they thought. They were part of my platoon. The guys thought it was funny, and they nicknamed me the Worm Man.

We had just dispersed, fanning out along a narrow perimeter of jungle. We were still in the free fire zone. In other words, anyone who lived there was considered the enemy.

I arrived about two months ago. Time had become disjointed. The jungle was getting inside me, in my blood, in my saliva, in my shit. It was eating me.

I wanted to be here. I wanted to sweat, I had dreamed of shooting, as an absolute, without connecting it to the idea of life or death. I wanted to do something. That was all. I wanted to be in my body and make it useful.

And now, I was casually letting myself disappear. I was getting blurred. Disembodied.

He emerged from the nighttime fog. Stumpy legs. Out of breath. I remember the rhythm of his shoulders, which reached toward the sky and then sank to the ground. Again. Again. Again. I don't know how long we stayed that way, looking at each other. But suddenly he lifted his arm toward me, splitting the sky. His arm seemed too long. He screamed. It was his voice that got me right in the stomach. It was like mine. It is strange to hear yourself scream.

So I fired. A hail of bullets. He fell. Got back up again. And he sunk into the night. I ran. I couldn't see him anymore. But I could smell him. My mouth started to water. The mouth of a predator. He couldn't escape me. We were like magnets.

My running was calculated and muffled, splitting the thick jungle. I had a goal: him.

The forest suddenly disappeared. It opened up under the

indigo sky. I could see only dark shapes I had narrowly avoided as I chased my prey.

Who was there, available and vulnerable, standing in front of me.

I had spotted him. I can even say that I looked at him. He was handsome. He had wide, dark eyes. Sunken cheeks and thick lips. He whispered something to me in Vietnamese.

And I fired. Into his stomach. Twice. He fell to his knees, gently. He sunk into the ground. In slow motion. He stayed like that for a moment. Kneeling, just looking at me. He was already dead, I think. But he didn't collapse. He wasn't surrendering. He stayed facing me, frozen in his savage dignity.

I would have liked him to fall. To surrender. To stop looking at me.

I approached him. I put my hand on his shoulder. It was thin, delicate. I pushed him. He slowly slid to the ground, face down.

I was finally able to lift my head. And I saw the village. The few scattered houses, outlined against the night.

The bodies creating stripes in space. Human stalactites hung from the trees, from the cornices, from the stars. Tens of hanging bodies. Raining down from the sky.

He had come to die with his people. He had run until he was underneath their absence like a blazing meteorite, holding back his fall until the end.

I think the wind came up, making the ropes around their necks swing. Like heavy pendulums, they marked the end of my world.

I collapsed on the ground.

I didn't move. For hours, maybe days.

Until my convoy found me, my body curled around my prey.

They sent me home. Back to my country, a 'Return to sender' label around my neck.

Gary Adams – Age 22

The door of the funeral home opens onto a generalized murmur, which you face, holding Gary's hand. He trembles less when he holds on to you.

You split the small crowd and eyes look you up and down. You go stand in front of your dead mother.

You haven't seen her in twenty-two years. She looks less severe than in your memory of her. Her prominent cheekbones dominate her face, casting their shadow on her hollow cheeks.

She is wearing lipstick. You had never seen her in makeup. You quickly remove it. You rub her thin lips with your fingertip.

Finally, your mother isn't unhappy. She is dead.

'Suzanne?'

You turn toward your father. Achilles. He is thinner, stooped, but his eyes are still sharp and deeply kind.

You tell him that your mother didn't wear lipstick. He answers that she should have. He extends his hand to Gary. The two men greet each other. Gary is a child. You feel it in your father's eyes.

Achilles hesitates. Then his body leans toward you. He takes you in his arms, which are still robust. Quickly. As if he were picking you. He wants to make sure he can take a piece of you before you disappear again.

Which you are ready to do.

Hiding in your wake, Gary follows you to the exit. Your sister Claire snarls at you as you pass. She is faded under her habit, and her firmness surprises you. She approaches you and asks to speak to you.

So in front of the funeral home, your veiled little sister brings you up to date. That François, your son, has run away. That he is sixteen years old. You notice her eyes watching Gary. Who could be the same age. She goes on. François left the foster home in Val d'Or where he grew up. The family of undertakers that took him in fell apart after the death of his adoptive mother.

François spent his childhood helping his new father embalm people. He learned to comb dead hair, to hem the dead's last pants, maybe to put a bit of lipstick on the mouth of a dead person who dreamed of wearing some.

The undertaker's new wife didn't like François. She beat him.

So François left the home.

'He wanted to find you.'

On the train on the way back to Montreal, you surprise yourself by looking outside, searching the passing countryside. Between the empty fields and the stripped forests, you are looking for your missing son.

Gary has monsters under his skin. He is extremely gentle, speaks little, smiles sometimes. He is in the habit of doing his hair by tracing a thin part down the right side of his delicate head. He rarely looks you in the eye. When he does, you make love. Or rather you make love to him. You wrap around him gently. Like a lullaby.

He comes alive at night. He gets up, breathless. Checks the deadbolt on the apartment once, then ten times. Seals the window with his fingertips to prevent the wind from reaching him. The wind makes him crazy.

You wait for it to pass. You serve him a drink, which he downs in one. He calms down a little. Enough so that you can pull him against you, where he huddles up. You like feeling his clammy skin against your breasts. He is short of breath, like a baby bird. You bandage his wounds with your long hands. You caress him. He goes back to sleep.

You share an apartment on Rue McGill in Montreal.

Books are lined along the hallway, awaiting their turn. Gary picks one at random and samples passages, feeding your desire to add to the collection.

And you go out for a few hours late in the afternoon, bringing him back a used book and a bottle of whisky.

While out on one of these forays, you find a job as a secretary at the railway workers' union on Rue Sainte-Catherine. A job that doesn't commit you to anything, which you do well and which you can quickly put out of your mind, going straight home to put all your energy into taking care of Gary.

Mousse is eighteen. She is a hostess at Expo '67. She is stunningly beautiful. Dark and slim.

A clay animal, fresh breezes, and plenty of cracks. Lava gushes from her wounds.

Mousse grew up with her aunts. She studied at boarding school, which she hated. Then she started studying communications at Université de Québec à Montréal.

One morning, she gets a call from Claire Meloche, her mother's sister.

She has found François, her little brother. Mousse hasn't seen him since they were separated.

Claire asks her if she wants to see him. Mousse says yes.

A run-down hospital. Several flights of stairs that Mousse slowly climbs. She is wearing a long skirt and laced boots. What do you wear for a reunion with your brother?

She tucks the stray strands of hair behind her ears.

'It's me.' 'It's Mousse.' 'I'm your sister.' 'Do you remember me?'

How do you introduce yourself to the one who was left behind?

Floors go by. Behind each door is thick glass. Faraway voices, the occasional scream. The smell of overcooked food and medication.

François is on the top floor.

'He has a view of the sky,' the lady at reception said kindly.

Mousse rings at the door. This one has bars. Not just anyone can enter the mental ward.

A man in a white coat comes to open it.

'I'm here to meet my little brother.'

Mousse enters the mental ward. There is compartmentalized chaos. Men and women who have stepped out of their bodies are spontaneously erupting. No one holds back, everyone is spilling over with something. Some are singing, others are crying, still others are yelling or laughing.

But there is natural light. And it's true that from here you can see the sky.

Mousse looks for François. Her little brother with the chubby cheeks and the incredibly long eyelashes.

But he is the one who finds her.

'Mousse?'

He recognizes her. Skinny and gaunt, tall and damaged, François walks toward his sister, ready to take her in his arms, his sister who has finally come back.

And in a sunny corner, with the sounds of the mad reverberating off them, Mousse and François tell each other about their lives.

He speaks in a voice that's all surface, a voice so soft that it can't help but soothe. François has taken refuge in the space in his head where he can't be hurt anymore. He tells Mousse that she looks like an angel. Mousse takes his hand. Fire and water meet, on the top floor of the tower of the insane. She is incandescent; he is aquatic. Each one has saved their skin as best they can.

Mousse strokes her little brother's rough cheeks.

He has put makeup on the dead and swallowed drugs.

He has fucked entire streets for warmth and money.

Now he hears voices. Sometimes gentle, sometimes angry.

He is so happy to be reunited with Mousse.

He shoves his hand in his pocket and takes out his wallet, from which he pulls an old piece of paper that has been folded and unfolded a thousand times over. With his long nails, he unfolds it.

A blue umbrella in a downpour.

Mousse leaves François in the sun.

Mousse has found her little brother. Now she can't die.

She will come back to visit him.

She will finish her drawing for him, which she will hang on the sterile walls of his room.

She will add a girl and a boy under the blue umbrella.

But it's too late to rescue him.

You take Gary in your arms and crack his shell. Even held like this, his body stays rigid for a moment, hunched, a painful implosion.

You start the music. Robert Charlebois. *Let me take you to my Boulé, my whistling river Boulé. Give me your hand and hang on tight, just run for a mile, on smooth rocks and logs, surrounded by water, watch you don't fall, give me your hand or you'll slip, watch you don't get wet!* And you dance. You dance with him pressed against you. You dance from your stomach and your loins. You dazzle him with your joyful, grounded strength. You are body to body, mouth to mouth, you pull him toward you. You make sure he is glued to the life he has left. *And the water the water whistling like a lamb pissing.*

Gary takes a bath, which you run for him. You make him spaghetti while he reads his second book of the day. You hear him laugh. It makes you feel unbelievably good.

The phone rings.

You answer. It's Mousse. She tells you she has found François. And that he wants to see you.

You feel trapped. The vice doesn't close around you but, rather, inside you. Your whole chest compresses.

You hang up.

The spaghetti is perfectly cooked.

Gary comes to curl up against you. Against your neck, your thighs, the folds of your body. He takes refuge there for a moment.

Sometimes his fingers travel along the tracks of your skin, spreading waves of shivers and stories of heroes moving through the dense jungle that is too vast for them.

Just like every afternoon for almost three years now, you go to the corner bookstore.

The shelf in the back is filled with used books. Classics, particularly mysteries, which Gary loves. You like sinking your nose into them before reading a few lines. From their smell, you can tell who has read them, and how many times. You can guess their age and their story.

You fill your arms with new stories, which allow your man to escape, to momentarily leave Vietnam, which is still eating away at him from the inside.

Your skin and the books will save him.

You pay. You keep just enough money for the daily bottle of whisky.

As you are leaving, the newspaper catches your eye. The face of Claude Gauvreau. Your friend from another life.

You grab the paper, clutching it, to read what is written. Claude killed himself. Jumped out of a window. He was impaled at the end of his fall.

He had just signed a contract with the Théâtre du Nouveau Monde, where his last play will be performed.

He was afraid of being loved.

You crumple your ranting friend's face, and you shove it in your pocket.

He gave a voice to the lost words that belonged to no one.

He has gone to find them.

The sun eats at your face. You walk with your fist gripped around the newspaper, Claude's face seeping into your palm. You would have liked to have said goodbye to him.

A man steps in front of you. He calls you Mom. You freeze.

As you confront his gentle, childlike features, you suit up. An invisible, sharp, metal cope covers you and protects you. You coldly study the image before you. Thin hair that the sun dusts and gets tangled in. A broad forehead that is older than the rest of the face. Huge, penetrating eyes.

With a subdued voice, François tells you that he is glad he found you. That he's been looking for you for a long time. He pulls a bit of change from his pocket, which he shows you in a naive gesture that unsettles you. He invites you for a coffee. He knows where you can get a good one that's cheap.

You tell him you're in a rush. You tell him you can't. You tell him that someone is waiting for you.

You don't tell him he is handsome. You don't tell him he should get his big coat cleaned and cut his long hair.

You disappear, trailing your heavy, rusted carapace behind you.

You go home without the bottle. You will go back out to get it. You need to hide away. In a cave where it will be easier for you to pretend.

You go home and head to your room, where you normally find Gary, curled up, awaiting your return. But he's not there. You go back to the kitchen, muttering his name.

'Gary?'

And you see him.

His long legs swaying in front of the window. His arms hanging limply down his body, having finally stopped trembling. His child's face is tilted to one side like the first time he looked at you. He is blue, suffocated, the rope firmly knotted around his broken neck.

You creep toward him, as if you might wake him.

You grab the chair that has toppled over; you stand on it and jam your fingers into the knotted lumps of the rope that has just killed the man you love. The one you couldn't save.

The one you grab hold of with both arms and lift to take to your bed where you hold him and rock him as you cry.

You failed again.

The police come the next morning to pronounce him dead. You spent your last night with him.

Now you're alone. Again.

1974–1981

You move. You leave everything behind. You find a room where you hang a hammock. You fill the fridge with booze, and you don't go out anymore.

You are forty-eight. And you don't give a shit about anything.

You get drunk and you fuck.

You fuck dirty. Only young men. Who you pick up in the street, in cafés, in bars. Because you smell like sex.

You invite them back to your place for a drink. You keep passing the bottle, you get undressed, you suck them off and you come.

You lose yourself in young flesh and become a landing place for thirsty male bodies.

Mousse has lost François. He left with nothing. Except a bag filled with teddy bears. He walks the streets with them. When night falls, he is rocked by his inner voices, a sacred circle that never leaves him on his own. François wants a family.

One morning his face appears in the window across the way. You are naked, holding a glass. And in front of you, an angelic face, framed with long grey hair, stares at you.

François has found you. He has rented the little alcove across the street from your house where, while he can't talk to you, at least he can look at you.

You stay like that for a moment, facing him. Your lost little boy. On the other side, his eyes are shining, and he smiles at you.

You smile back. As best you can. Your smile muscles seem to have atrophied, and it requires a super-human effort. You smile at him because you know that you will never be able to forgive yourself. You know that the forgiveness you have to beg for is simply too great.

You close the curtains on the face of your son, whom you haven't touched in twenty years.

And perhaps to feel closer to him, you go mad too.

You are hot and cold. You feel like you're being tracked by a pack of lame wolves.

They lock you up.

You share a hospital room with a young woman, whose moaning cuts through the night.

You know that everyone is talking about you behind your back. You glare at them and shout that you understand everything.

They take care of you. You let them. You need someone to take care of you.

Your sister Claire comes to your bedside and strokes your hair. She tells you that you will get out soon, if you listen to the doctors.

Her voice reaches you as an echo, and you cover your ears. You're tired.

Claire dims the light in your little room. She holds out a glass of water to you. She waits for you to calm down. And she tells you that your daughter, Mousse, is giving birth.

Just a few floors away.

You wait for night to fall. You swap your hospital gown for a white smock.

You run your hands through your hair and put a bit of blush on your cheeks.

You feel diffuse, dissipated in the medicated air of the mad. You are swept along in a foggy momentum. Nothing like courage, but a gentle force that moves you toward the few steps to climb to your daughter.

You cross the maternity ward on tiptoe. Something inside you is whispering that you have the right to be there.

At reception, you ask for Madame Barbeau's room.

They point the way, and you follow it with your head held high. You knock and go in.

It's the woman you see first. Your spirited daughter. Her eyes bore into you, pierce you, crucify you.

She calls you Mom. And this time you answer yes. Without even hesitating.

'It's a girl,' she tells you.

You are happy. On an impulse, you approach her, a lump of joy caught in your throat.

Your grown-up daughter looks away from you to cover her child.

Round and still warm, she is resting in her arms as if they had been custom made for her. She feeds hungrily, already very much alive.

Every part of you that was floating comes slowly down to the ground. You take root again in spite of yourself. You drink from this spring of pain; for a moment you are back in your forgotten body.

The child is now resting on her breast. Mousse briefly raises her eyes.

She studies you from a distance. Remembers only the void left in your wake.

The perfume of your absence is stronger than the perfume on your throat. She will live on that smell of emptiness, planning her days so that they are always full.

You are proud of your daughter. She has won. She has created a next chapter for all of you, which she will spend her whole life writing.

You have the impression that Mousse is clutching the newborn in her arms. That she will not let you approach. But her voice rises from somewhere deep down and asks you, while tightening her embrace, if you want to hold the baby.

So you lean over and gently undo the loving knots, raising one of your daughter's delicate arms, then the other, and you take me in your cold hands.

You lift me to your chest. I look like Mousse.

You are twenty-five again, and you feel the desire for new beginnings.

You have let your life go by, impenetrable to the world.

Mousse holds her arms out to you, and you want to give her back everything you took away.

You place me in the crook of her arm, and you leave the room, a bit of you lingering in the air and on our skin.

You made a hole in my mother, and I'm the one who will fill it.

1981–2009

You live like a hermit in a high-rise building. Buddha and the Rideau Canal outside your window are practically your only companions.

You practice meditation. You try to leave your body, which you can no longer stand.

You have gone back to hide out in Ottawa. You shave your head. You dissolve into the air.

You practice zazen, which advocates a return to oneself, and it comforts you in your reclusion.

You find a spiritual master in the States. You write to him, 'I believe that at this point in my life the answer is: now as the only path.'

You plunge your hands into soil, transplant bulbs that you then water. They don't grow, but you keep trying.

You cook, something you have never really done. You chop vegetables with the precision of an assassin. You leave under your nails the earth that you used to hold in contempt and that now keeps you connected to life.

You don't talk to anyone, but you pour out fragments of your daily life to your spiritual master. You write to him that you want to devote the rest of your life to Buddhism.

And you are pleased with your tofu-stuffed peppers.

And in a postscript that reveals the extent of your solitude, you say, 'My little pepper plant is doing well.'

You water your plant and watch it grow slowly in front of your curtainless window.

The little plant growing in the sun connects you to the living.

You work not to dry up. You survive.

One morning, all the way downstairs, an old woman runs around the building. You see her pass under your balcony then disappear, then reappear, always running.

This ungainly break in the stillness makes you burst out laughing, and you abandon yourself to it for a moment.

In the Borduas archives, an old, moth-eaten manuscript is belatedly found. *Les Aurores Fulminantes*, by Suzanne Meloche.

Your poems are submitted to the publisher Les Herbes Rouges, where twenty-nine years after they were born, they are finally published.

You don't go to the launch. You are busy meditating, surrounded by your plants which barely grow.

But you clip the few reviews anyway, which you keep between the pages of a book, in your bookcase.

Les Herbes Rouges occasionally publishes older texts that time has forgotten or that were never published, like those of Suzanne Meloche, whose poems, collected under the title Les Aurores Fulminantes *in issue 78 of the magazine, date back to 1949. They have not aged in those thirty years, and in reading them one regrets that their author did not publish them at the time and follow them up with at least a half dozen more. Suzanne Meloche is part of a generation of water diviners and sorcerers that made our right to free speech possible, often paying dearly for it.*

Review of *Aurores Fulminantes* in
Le livre d'ici, vol. 5, no. 41, July 16, 1980.

Les Aurores Fulminantes (no. 78), *written in 1949, highly syntactic verse, fantasies of cracks, crevices, dents, steep slopes, a restraint that makes it all spill over; a piece of work that should not fear posterity. A surreal code, but one that hasn't aged. 'Here is the back of my hand/like a liqueur.'*

Review of *Aurores Fulminantes*, Joseph Bonenfant,
Le Devoir, July 30, 1980.

One morning, the phone rings. That never happens anymore, or at least rarely. You have burned all your bridges.

It's Mousse. She wanted to know if you were still alive.

Your mouth is dry. You tell her that you would rather not talk to her. You hang up.

That night, you don't sleep.

You get up and kneel before Buddha. You close your eyes. Deep in the *You* that you want to purify, there is a black hole. It is sucking you in.

The next morning, you take the train to Montreal.

You walk along Rue Champagneur, hands jammed in the pockets of your long coat.

A little girl climbs the mountain of snow in front of her house. She is solidly built and plants her feet in the ice on the way to the summit, which she is proud to reach.

'I did it!'

Her mother joins her, doing her best to pull a sled with a baby bundled up in it.

For a brief moment, you are thrust back into the past. It is like seeing yourself. Walking through the hard winter, your children making you feel like you're dressed in your Sunday best, like a crown too heavy to bear.

Mousse applauds the little queen of the hill, who slides down to her. The three of them go up the few steps that separate them from their home, from the man who is heating it, from the family they have managed to build, despite it all, despite you. The door closes behind them, without them noticing you.

Your feet are frozen and your stomach is in a knot. You slowly cross the street to put a small booklet from Les Herbes Rouges in your daughter's mailbox: your *Aurores Fulminantes*, what remains of you.

You hastily scratched out on the very first page, 'To Mousse. We went too far, too fast.'

You leave, believing this to be goodbye.

But upstairs, in the third-floor window, the little girl watches you head off into the distance. You catch her eye. Lift a hesitant hand toward her.

I stare at you without responding. You hurt my mother, and I don't like you.

That year, my mother makes a film about the children of the signatories of the *Refus Global*. It is a personal quest that leads her to the children of Riopelle, Ferron, and Borduas. All of them missing their parents.

It will be a difficult year for her, and one that will transform her.

That same year, she will be reunited with her little brother again.

He lives in a residence in Quebec City. A psychiatric facility where he has his room, where one hundred baptised stuffed animals lay on his bed, where he chain smokes, looking out the window as time passes slowly on the majestic river.

He didn't take care of his smile, which is of no use to anyone. His teeth are black, and his beard is long.

He is a music lover. And very cultivated. He speaks in a voice softer than the first snow and has the tender, deep eyes of someone special.

He spends Christmas with his sister. In the country house with the red roof, where, later, your ashes will lend substance to the wind.

François still believes in Santa Claus. He enjoys preparing the snack that will be left under the tree for him. Dates and a glass of red wine. He teams up with the children, a guest in their world, the one he missed and that now sweeps over him like an illness.

François makes holes in the snow, all around the house, into which he sets candles, sheltered from the wind. Mousse follows him and lights a ribbon of lights in the middle of the country. Santa Claus won't forget her little brother.

For a number of years, Manuel, my brother, keeps calling you. He has a keen sense of connection, as if he had grown up the reverse of you. And even though every time he runs headlong into your cold, distant voice and you refuse to meet him, he calls back. And in his child's voice, then his young man's voice, he repeats that he wants to meet the person who brought his mother into the world.

You stand up straight in front of the wall of little mailboxes. You don't want to be one of those old people with the sad, stooped backs waiting for the mail.

As your eyes distractedly travel across the other boxes, they hit upon a name, scribbled by hand: STRIKE, HILDA. #405.

You freeze, stunned. Hilda Strike? On the floor above yours?

You open your mailbox. You find a parcel in it, which you pick up like a burning ember that's about to send the building, the city, and the country up in flames.

You can't imagine where it comes from. Nothing and no one has made it into your den in years. You live on incense and vodka. You read, and you talk to Buddha.

You rush into the elevator, holding the parcel away from your body. It scares you.

On the fourth floor, the elevator door opens, and there she is. Hilda. A cane in hand, running shoes on her feet.

'Going down?'

You are speechless. Her black, keen eyes. The eyes of a fox. Her delicate eyebrows, shaped into a triangle, her wide, wrinkled forehead, her grey hair pulled back elegantly in a bun that will soon be undone by the wind. And a large necklace that weighs down her chest.

She gets in. The elevator continues its journey, rising toward the top floor.

She sighs: she wanted to go down. You apologize. She interrupts you by turning her sharp eyes on you and leaning heavily into each word as she utters it.

'Don't be sorry.'

You smile.

Going back to your apartment, you tell yourself that for the first time in a long time, you may have found a friend.

You drop the package on the coffee table and wait until evening to open it. A sudden rift in the evening: it's a white dressing gown. Immaculate.

Accompanied by a note from Mousse, carefully drafted.

She dreamed of you. That she gave you a white dress as a gift.

You undress. The reflection of your tired body makes you smile. It has been desired and thoroughly explored. But no one ever possessed it. Except, once, your children.

You shake out the dressing gown, and it unfurls in front of you.

You drape it over your shoulders and slip your arms in, casually wrapping it around you. Knot it at the waist to seal it tight. You are trapped in a gift that came too abruptly, that is too white, that burns your skin.

You rip the page from a notebook and jot down the words you need.

'Thank you, Mousse. The dressing gown fits me; it's just the right length. Very pretty. Don't send anything else. Suzanne – Mom.'

It's the first and last time you write that word.

2006. There are three knocks at your door. You don't answer.

You settle in to your well-honed immobility.

Three more insistent knocks.

You put on your dressing gown. You take the time to line your eyes with black kohl. And you open the door.

At first you don't understand the human forms taking shape in front of you. You need time to make out the features of your daughter, and the similar ones of your granddaughter. It's like looking in a mirror with no mercy.

You adjust the knot on your dressing gown. You hesitate between closing and opening the door you are holding on to.

You swallow a wisp of air, which they have brought in from the outside. You ask them how they got in. Normally you have to ring the buzzer downstairs and announce yourself.

They snuck in. Knowing perfectly well that you wouldn't open the door for them. They took advantage of the fact that a woman went running out the door.

They have pairs of skates slung around their neck and just stopped by.

You don't decide to open the door, but you do. My mother and I go in. We sit on your sofa. Facing you.

And you decide to soak up the scene, which will not be repeated. First timidly, then more and more hungrily, you take us in with your eyes. Your eyes roam over our features, like over forgotten drawings you have done.

You ask us what brings us to Ottawa. We each have a different reason. It is pure coincidence that we were going there at the same time. You don't really listen to what we are saying, but rather to the music of our voices.

You abandon yourself to the pleasure of our refreshing singsong.

Your eyes wander over the prominent foreheads and the streamlined mouths. And the long fingers made for the piano. Your mother's fingers.

You offer us a cup of tea, which you calmly prepare, aware of the magnitude of the moment. You are a grandmother making tea for her daughter and granddaughter.

We drink and you watch us.

You try to tell us about your dull, indistinguishable days. You seem almost normal.

Then Mousse asks you why. Why did you leave?

You disconnect and try to hang on to the stubby shadow of your plant that is trying to take the sky by storm.

You have nothing to say about that.

We are trapped in the silence.

We decide to leave.

You close the door behind us. You lock it with the key.

On your sofa, the imprints of our bodies gradually disappear. You lie down on them.

You swallow the void that rushes into your chest, like the ocean rushing into the drowned.

You pick up the phone and call Mousse. She is skating on the frozen canal that runs alongside your control tower.

'Never do that again.'

In spring 2009, you receive an invitation from Les Herbes Rouges. As part of the tenth poetry market and the fortieth anniversary of their publishing house, a reading has been organized in a tent, in front of Mont Royal metro.

Fashionable authors will read surreal poems from the past and present. Including yours, which will be read for the first time.

You are eighty-three.

You carefully place the invitation between the pages of a book, and you open a bottle of vodka.

Two glasses in hand, you leave your apartment.

Apartment 405. You knock. Hilda opens the door. You don't say anything; she invites you to sit down.

Settled into a purple velvet armchair, you scan the walls while she is busy in the kitchen.

There are pictures of her everywhere, running. Young, with short, wavy hair, Bermuda shorts hiked up above her belly button.

She joins you in the living room, hands you a plate of spaghetti and meat sauce. You fill the glasses with vodka again. You toast, your old hands wrapped around the slender glasses.

You don't talk much, comfortable in this quiet new association. You feel special being able to see her motionless. She eats and drinks with long, slow gestures, sometimes lifting her eyes to you, which you meet, delighted, mollified.

That evening, you learn that the necklace she wears around her neck, which hangs down to her chest, weighs exactly four hundred and twelve grams. The weight of a gold medal.

She tells you what you already know, and you are careful not to interrupt her, enjoying hearing the tale from her own mouth.

Her event was the women's hundred-metre dash.

'They used to call me the ostrich,' she says, a flash of pride in her eyes.

In 1932, competing at the Los Angeles Olympic Games, she won the silver, beaten by Stella Walsh. She makes a face when she says her name.

And for you, she reminisces about the splendour of the race, her smooth start, her phenomenal propulsion, the powerful conviction that she would get the gold, and the second that relegated her to the sidelines of history.

She takes a last mouthful of spaghetti, and she seems to have a hard time swallowing.

Then, in a few words, still bitter, the reversal of destiny, years later: Stella Walsh, who won by a few centimetres, wasn't a woman.

'Hermaphrodite. They found out when she died.'

Hilda downs her vodka in one.

'Still waiting for my medal.'

She mechanically adjusts the necklace around her neck. And then you see. Her bent neck, her swollen ankles. The apartment of a lonely old woman who ran all of her life. And yet no one remembers her today.

And you are overcome.

That night, you write your will by hand, on a blank sheet of paper.

You put the names of your children on it. Then mine, and my brother's.

On that evening in particular, you want us to remember you.

In front of the Mont Royal metro, I am listening to your poems bursting with vitality, while you put on your makeup. A thick line of kohl under your still alert pupils. Naked facing the mirror, you take in your round, barren body. Slowly, you run your tired hand over your lifeless sex. You close your eyes and settle into the waves of your breath. You rock as pleasure rises to your stomach.

You come, eyes open, staring at your reflection. You grant yourself a pardon.

And you let yourself slide along the cold bathroom floor.

December 23, 2009, wrapped in your white dressing gown.

We are your sole heirs. So, finally, you are inviting us over. We have to go empty your little apartment.

We set out into winter to meet you. Through the snow. Archaeologists of a murky life.

At your apartment, we are on our hands and knees, searching. Your closet. Hats. Dresses. Lots of black clothes.

I can't help but plunge my nose into the fabric. Smells are usually so revealing. But even they are furtive. Subtle, faint, hard to pin down. An accidental blend of incense, the sweat of days spent not moving. A subtle note of alcohol, perhaps?

In a shoebox there are pictures of us: me and my brother, at every age. You kept them. And my mother kept sending them to you year after year. Our ages are written on the back, traces of time lost, wasted, slipped away. It's your loss.

My mother is sitting in your rocking chair. Gently, she touches you. Rests her hands where you rested yours. Rocks to the rhythm of a lullaby, the one she never heard.

I find your red red lipstick in the small bathroom. And short sticks of kohl, which you lined your eyes with, giving them power. I draw a line under mine.

My mother finds a piece of furniture, made by her father a long time ago. We take it down to the car. She takes the rocking chair too, carrying it on her back, and my father lashes it securely to the roof.

We're leaving soon. I'm in your room. There is a small green plant in the window. It is leaning against the pane, drawn to the day.

Books are piled by the foot of your bed. I read a few passages at random, suddenly greedy for clues about you.

I find a yellowed cardboard folder between two books on Buddhist zazen.

It contains letters. Poems. Newspaper articles.

A gold mine, which I stuff into my bag like a thief.

We're leaving. I slip a worn copy of *Thus Spoke Zarathustra* into my pocket.

We close your door behind us, forever.

We drive slowly through the storm. On the roof, the rocking chair cuts through the wind, heroically. I don't know it yet, but I will rock my children in it.

I flip through Nietzsche, yellowed with age. There is a laminated newspaper article stuck between two pages.

The picture of a burning bus.

1961, Alabama.

In bold type: *Freedom riders: political protest against segregation.*

Around the bus are young Black people and White people, in shock, refugees from the flames. A young woman is on her knees. She looks like me.

A huge field, under a stormy sky. A woman is standing. She is taking root.

It's painful.

She makes a hole. She wants it to be deep.

The woman is my mother.

She is throwing your ashes in the ground.

A handful of you gets away from her and flies into the wind. She works faster. You won't get away from her.

Your daughter is planting you behind her house, in a huge field that she knows by heart, in the space where she takes her morning constitutionals and her evening walks.

The black sky above swallows you both up.

She works furiously in the rain. She mixes you with the soil.

Where she knows she will be able to find you.

It's over.

You can't run anymore.

Present day

It's five in the morning. The sun is rising over the countryside, an ardent green. My newborn daughter wakes up at that mysterious hour, in the in-between part of the day.

I take her for a walk along the dirt road. Nestled in my arms, she takes in the morning air like a huge surprise. Her entire body opens up at the slightest breeze. This moving encounter with the world marks our humble procession; we are coming to see you.

At the end of the field, a long flat stone sits among the pines. The names of my ancestors are engraved on it. Under those of my father's loving parents, my mother engraved yours. Your name, its letters carved into the grey stone.

My mother, broken-hearted. The shards of glass left forever under her skin, traces of the abandonment she carries like a coat of arms.

My mother who doesn't believe she can be loved. To hug her, to pull her into your arms, you have to hone your technique.

She is a grandmother four times over. She still lives with my father.

Together they are resistance fighters, builders, alchemists.

I cross the damp morning field. We stand before you.

The names written above yours have counted in my life. So why you? Why do I seek you out to tell my stories to?

At my feet is a circle of flattened grass, preserved by the dew. A deer came by in the night and curled up in the shadow of your grave. I sit on its bed, my daughter tucked in my arms.

The sun comes up, licking the horizon.

Because I am made partly from your desertion. Your absence is part of me, and it shaped me. You are the one to whom I owe the murky water that feeds my roots, which run deep.

So you continue to exist.

In my unquenchable thirst to love.

And in my need to be free, like an absolute necessity.

But free with them.
I am free together, me.

My daughter has fallen asleep at my breast.

The two of us as one before the majestic forest, under the immense sky, where the wild clouds appear, we are together and we salute you, Suze.

I remember you.

We will remember you.

The following notes provide context to some of the documents, laws, and movements that were shaping Quebec toward the mid-20th century and that are mentioned in this novel.

Programme de restauration sociale: A program for social recovery published in Quebec in 1933 by a group of priests and laypeople that focused on nationalism and corporatism and formed the basis for future radical electoral platforms by Quebec political parties. It combined traditional values with more progressive measures, such as assistance for the unemployed and nationalized financial and utility monopolies.

Refus global: A manifesto published in 1948 by members of the Automatist movement. The main essay was written by artist Paul-Émile Borduas, criticizing Quebec's traditional, religious-based values and calling for liberation, an international outlook, and hope.

Les Automatistes: A group of dissident artists based in Montreal in the 1940s, engaging in visual arts, theatre, poetry, and dance. Founded by painter Paul-Émile Borduas, the group was influenced by Surrealism's theory of automatism, which involves suppressing conscious control of the creative process.

L'Action catholique: A rural daily paper published between 1915 and 1962, to give the faithful guidance in everyday life.

The Padlock Law: Enacted in 1937, a statute that allowed buildings deemed used for propagating communism to be closed for one year.

The excerpt from *Maldoror* on page 65 is from:
Comte de Lautréamont. *Lautréamont's Maldoror*. Translated by
    Alexis Lykiard. New York: Allison & Busby, 1970, pp. 98-99.

The excerpt from *Bien-être* on pages 87-88 is from:
Claude Gauvreau. *The Good Life*. Translated by Ray Ellenwood.
    Toronto: Coach House Press, 1981, p. 42.

The excerpt from *Refus Global/Total Refusal* on pages 108 and 151
is from:
The Canadian Encyclopedia online, consulted April 2017.

THE AUTHOR'S ACKNOWLEDGEMENTS

Thank you to my grandfather, Marcel, for giving me permission.

Thank you to my mother for doing the same. And for reliving all of this for me.

Thank you to Louise-Marie Lacombe, private detective and prospector, without whom I wouldn't have been able to find Suzanne and invent her to my liking.

Thank you to art historian François-Marc Gagnon. His beautifully written *Chroniques du movement automatiste québécois* nourished me, from the beginning to the end.

Thank you to Peter Byrne, found in an Italian oasis, for all of his stories, driven by a profound love for my grandmother.

Thank you to François Barbeau, Ninon Gauthier, Guy Meloche, Marielle Brisebois Meloche, Claire Meloche, Madeleine Meloche, Brigitte Meloche, Anne-Marie Rainville, Andrée Pion, Suzanne Hamel, Pâquerette Villeneuve, and the family and friends of Gary Adams.

Thank you to everyone who remembered Suzanne for me.

Thank you to Maj, for the elegance.

Thank you to Jean-Marc Dalpé, Daniel Poliquin, and Raymond Cloutier for their advice.

And a big thanks to Émile, my man, for every part of you, sharing every part of my whole life. To Philippe and Manon, my parents. And to Danielle, Dounia, Maryse, Jules, Marie-T, Monique, who allowed me to be both a mother and a writer.

Born in 1979, and named an Artist for Peace in 2012, **Anaïs Barbeau-Lavalette** has directed several award-winning documentary features. She has also directed two fiction features: *Le Ring* (2008), *Inch'allah* (2012, which received the Fipresci Prize in Berlin). She is the author of the travelogue *Embrasser Yasser Arafat* (2011) and the novels *Je voudrais qu'on m'efface* (2010) and *La femme qui fuit* (Prix des libraires du Québec, Prix France-Québec, Prix de la ville de Montréal), garnering both critical and popular success.

Rhonda Mullins is a writer and translator living in Montreal. She won the 2015 Governor General's Literary Award for Translation for Jocelyne Saucier's *Twenty-One Cardinals*. *And the Birds Rained Down*, her translation of Saucier's *Il pleuvait des oiseaux*, was a cbc Canada Reads Selection for 2015. It was also shortlisted for the Governor General's Literary Award, as were her translations of Louis Carmain's *Guano*, Élise Turcotte's *Guyana* and Hervé Fischer's *The Decline of the Hollywood Empire*.

Typeset in Jenson.

Printed at the Coach House on bpNichol Lane in Toronto, Ontario, on Zephyr Antique Laid paper, which was manufactured, acid-free, in Saint-Jérôme, Quebec, from second-growth forests. This book was printed with vegetable-based ink on a 1973 Heidelberg KORD offset litho press. Its pages were folded on a Baumfolder, gathered by hand, bound on a Sulby Auto-Minabinda and trimmed on a Polar single-knife cutter.

Translated by Rhonda Mullins
Edited and designed by Alana Wilcox
Cover design by Ingrid Paulson
Photo of Rhonda Mullins by Owen Egan

Coach House Books
80 bpNichol Lane
Toronto ON M5S 3J4
Canada

416 979 2217
800 367 6360

mail@chbooks.com
www.chbooks.com